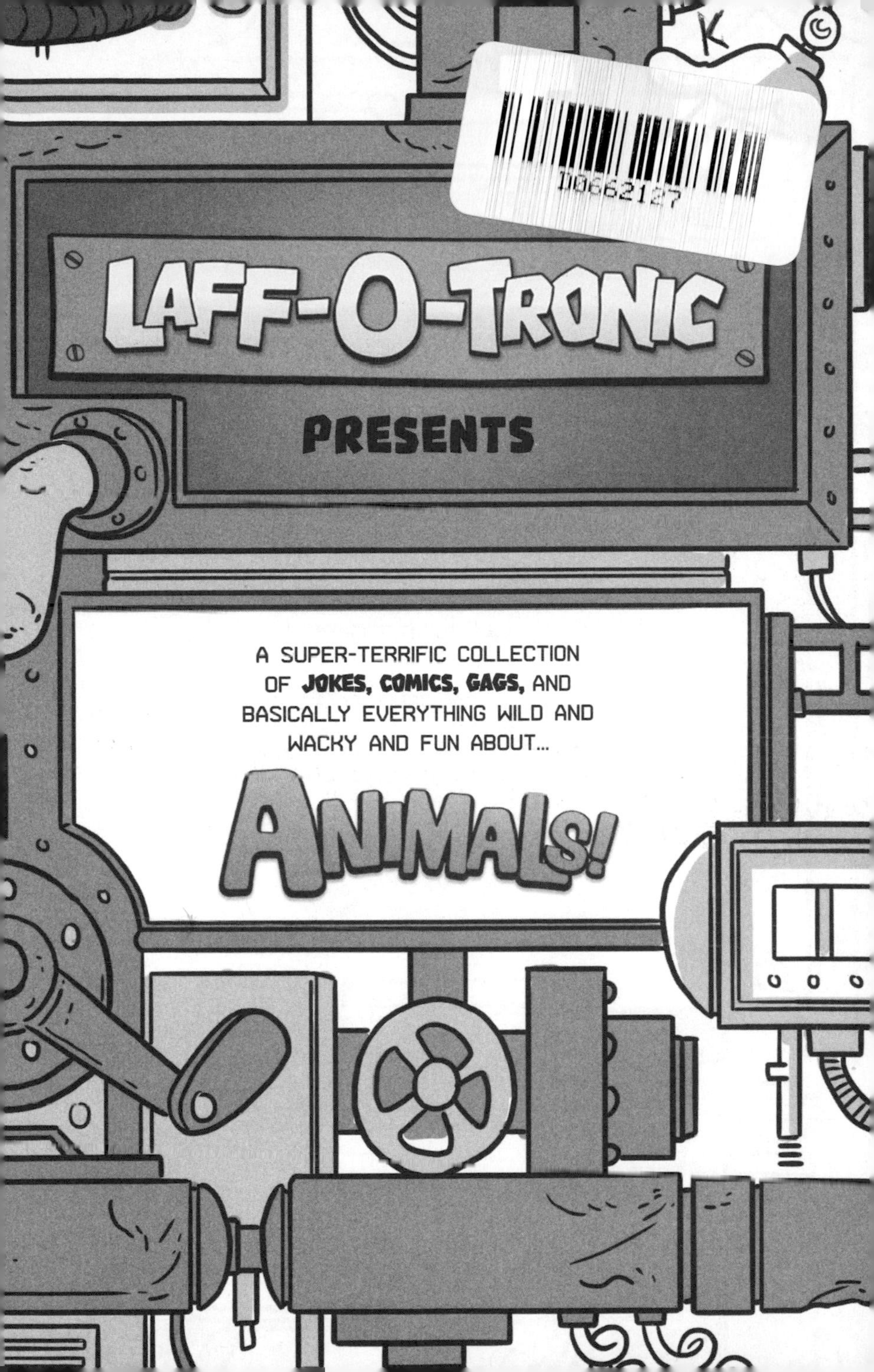
LAFF-O-TRONIC
PRESENTS
A SUPER-TERRIFIC COLLECTION OF JOKES, COMICS, GAGS, AND BASICALLY EVERYTHING WILD AND WACKY AND FUN ABOUT...
ANIMALS!

BORING STUFF...

LAFF-O-TRONIC JOKE BOOKS! IS PUBLISHED
BY STONE ARCH BOOKS, A CAPSTONE IMPRINT
1710 ROE CREST DRIVE
NORTH MANKATO, MN 56003
WWW.CAPSTONEYOUNGREADERS.COM

CATALOGING-IN-PUBLICATION DATA IS AVAILABLE
ON THE LIBRARY OF CONGRESS WEBSITE.
ISBN: 978-1-4342-6020-8 (LIBRARY HARDCOVER)
ISBN: 978-1-4342-6190-8 (PAPERBACK)

DESIGNER: RUSSELL GRIESMER
EDITOR: DONALD LEMKE

PRINTED IN THE UNITED STATES OF AMERICA
IN THE STEVENS POINT, WISCONSIN.
032013   007227WZF13

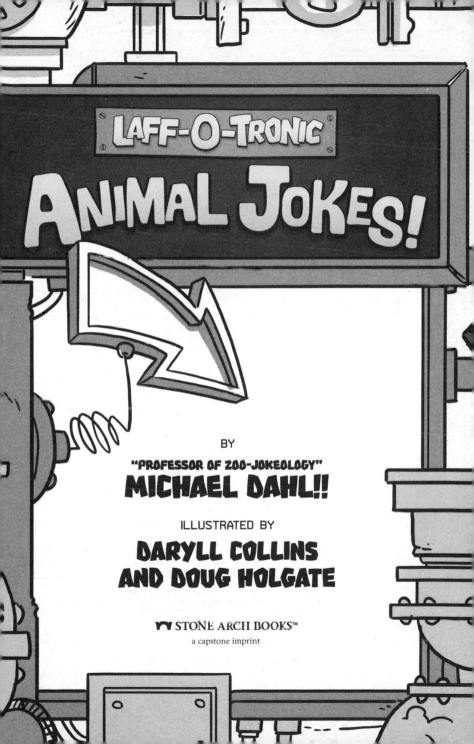

LAFF-O-TRONIC

ANIMAL JOKES!

BY

"PROFESSOR OF ZOO-JOKEOLOGY"
MICHAEL DAHL!!

ILLUSTRATED BY

**DARYLL COLLINS
AND DOUG HOLGATE**

STONE ARCH BOOKS™
a capstone imprint

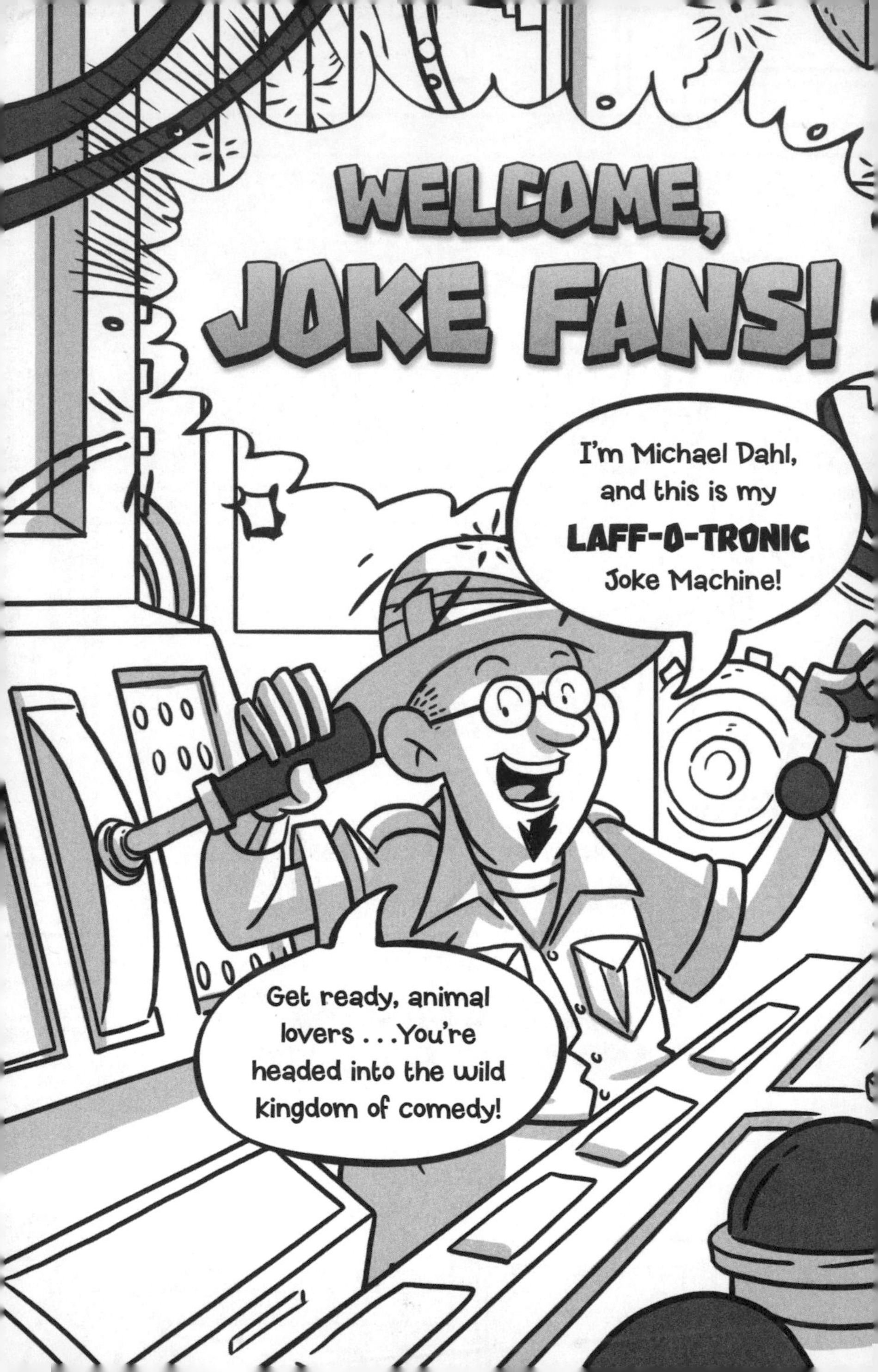
WELCOME, JOKE FANS!
I'm Michael Dahl, and this is my LAFF-O-TRONIC Joke Machine!
Get ready, animal lovers . . . You're headed into the wild kingdom of comedy!

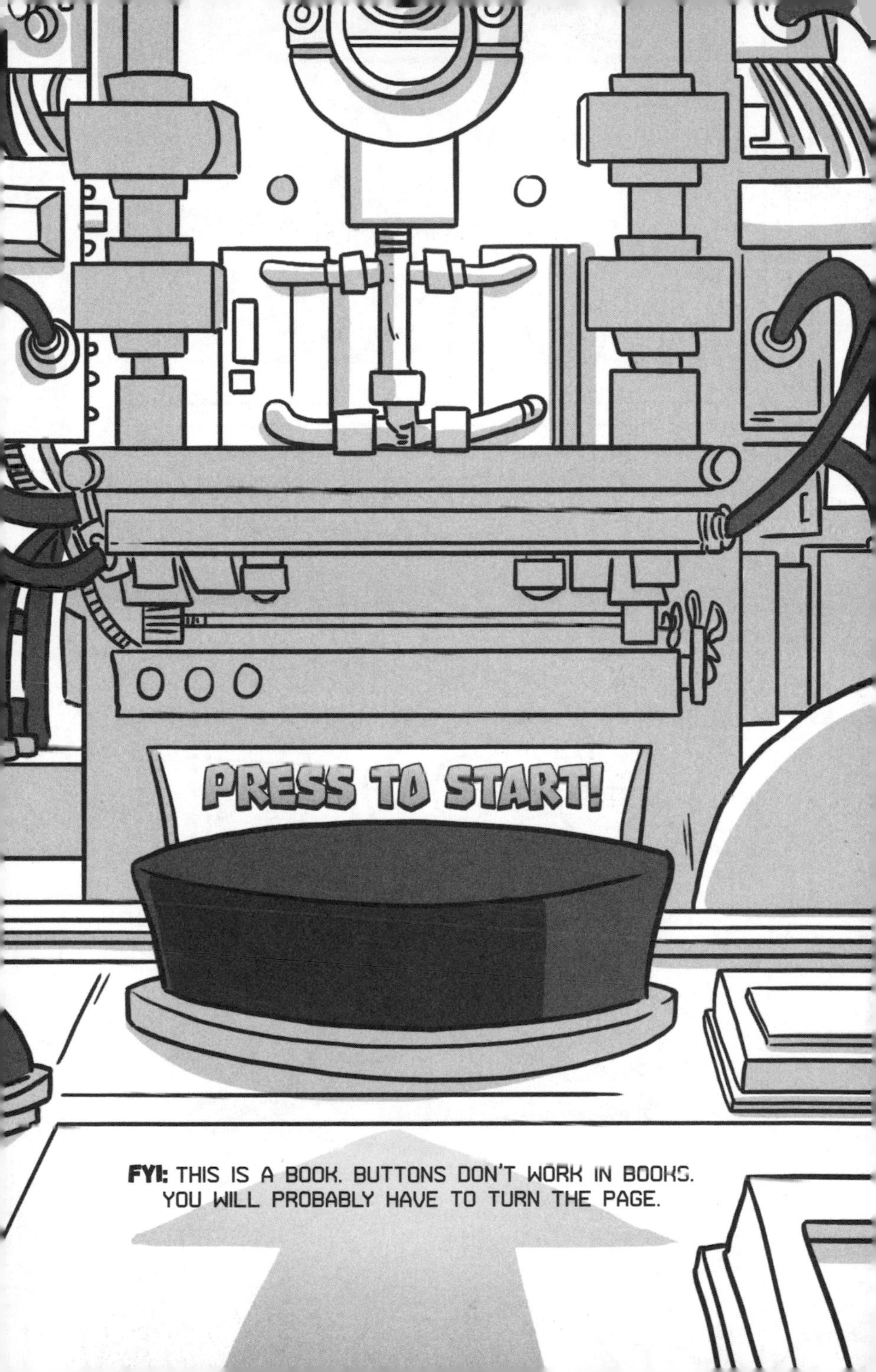
PRESS TO START!
FYI: THIS IS A BOOK. BUTTONS DON'T WORK IN BOOKS. YOU WILL PROBABLY HAVE TO TURN THE PAGE.

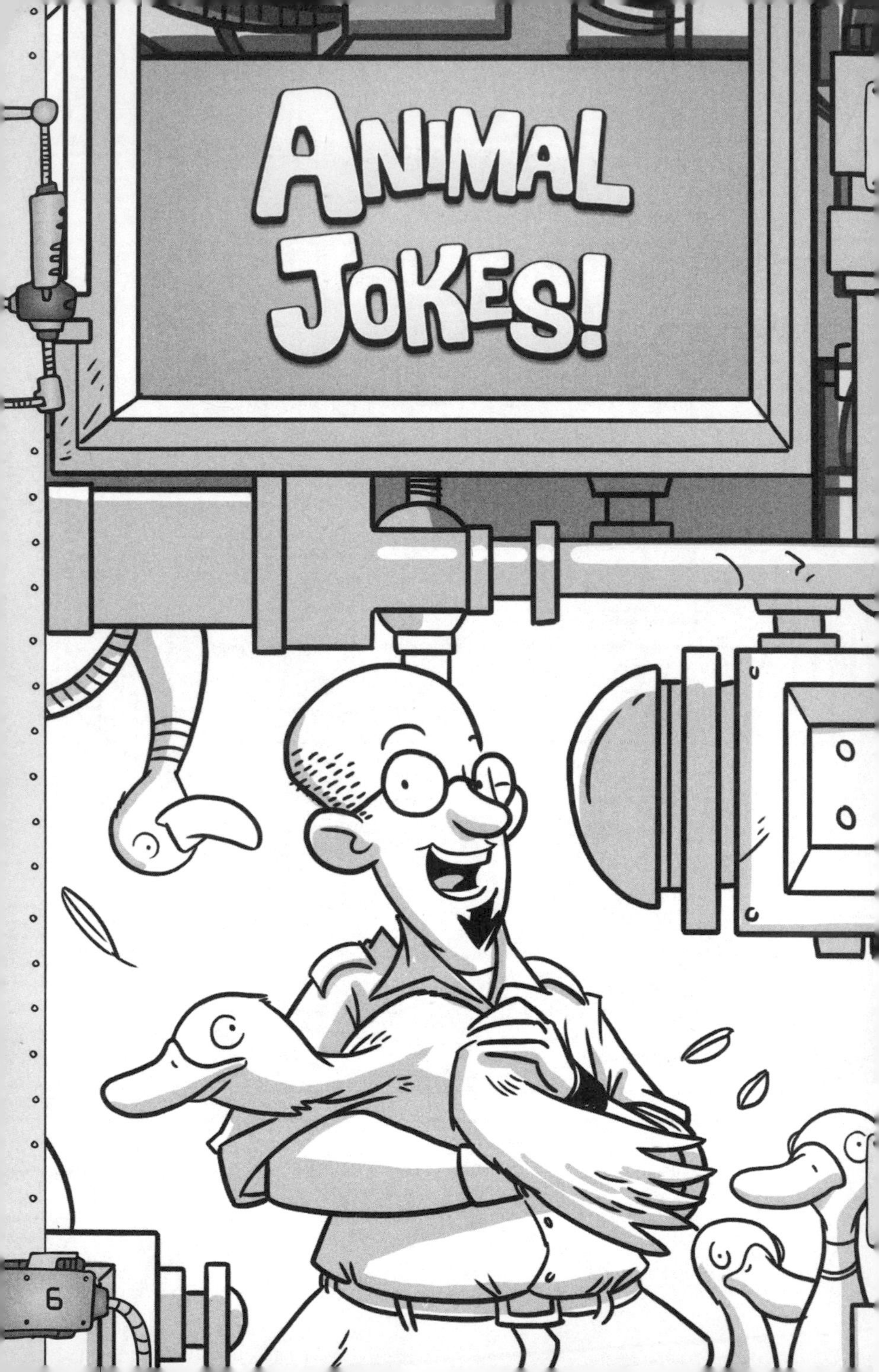
ANIMAL JOKES!

What do cats like to eat for dessert?
Mice-cream cones!

**What do you call an octopus
that robs banks?**
Billy the Squid.

What's the furriest side of a kitten?
The outside!

**What do you give a dog
with a fever?**
Mustard. It's the best thing for
a hot dog. (Maybe relish, too!)

Where do polar bears keep their money?
In a snow bank.

Where do otters come from?
Otter space!

What day do fish hate the most?
Fryday!

Why do hummingbirds hum?
Because they forgot the words!

How did the little bee get to school?
He took the buzz.

What do bees chew for fun?
Bumble gum!

What do you do with a blue whale?
Try to cheer it up!

How can you tell if an octopus is parked in your driveway?

From the squid-marks.

Why didn't the crab share his toys with his little brother?

Because he was a little shellfish.

What do you call a koala without any socks on?

Bearfoot.

How can you tell that carrots are good for your eyes?

Have you ever seen a rabbit wearing glasses?

What does a dog put into his doghouse?

Fur-niture.

What does a bee order at McDonald's?

A humburger.

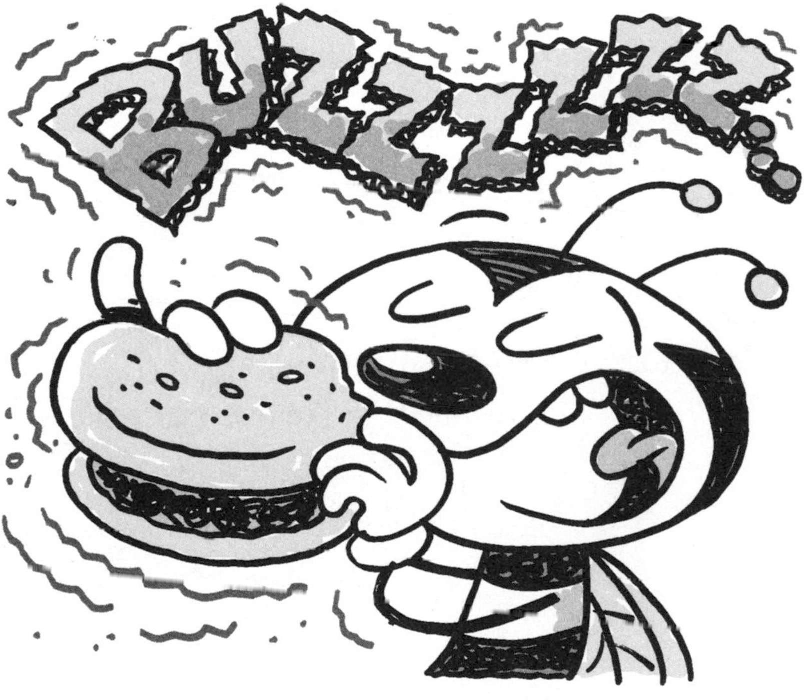
BUZZZZZ...

What do you get if you cross a kitten with a tree?

A cat-a-log.

What kind of cat is the most helpful?

A first aid kit.

Why didn't Noah fish very much?

He only had two worms.

Did you hear about the two silkworms that had a race?

They wound up in a tie!

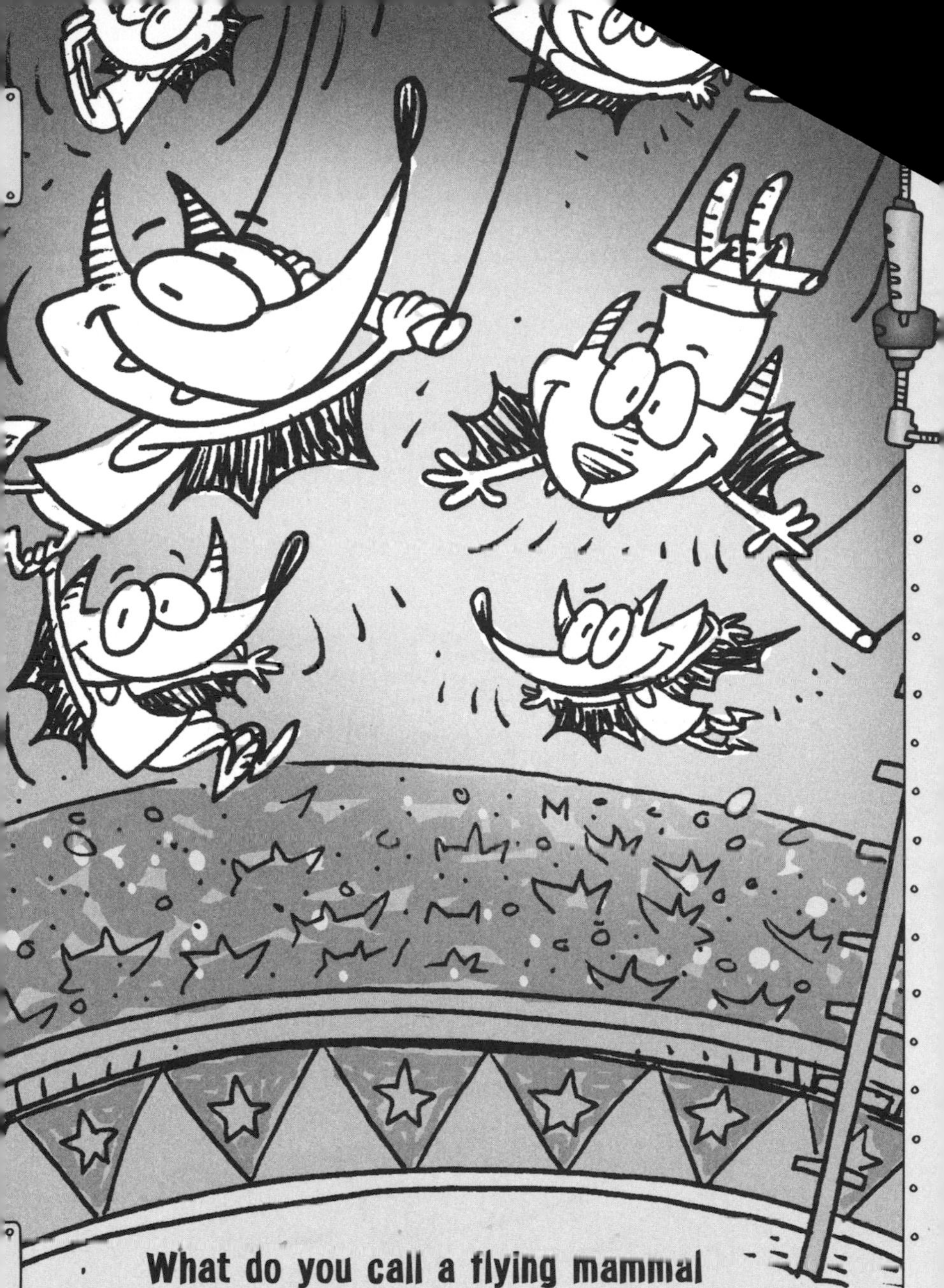

What do you call a flying mammal that works in the circus?

An acro-bat!

What did the cat do after it ate a hunk of cheese?

It waited by the mouse hole with baited breath.

What happened when the lion ate the clown?

He felt funny.

What did the duck say when it bought some lipstick?

"Just put it on my bill."

How do cats learn about the world?
They watch the evening mews.

**What kind of dog can cook
dinner for its owner?**
An oven mutt.

What kinds of dogs are like short skirts?
Peekin' knees.

**What did the Dalmatian say
after dinner?**
"That hit the spots!"

**Why did the little kid bring a book
to the zoo?**
He liked reading between the lions.

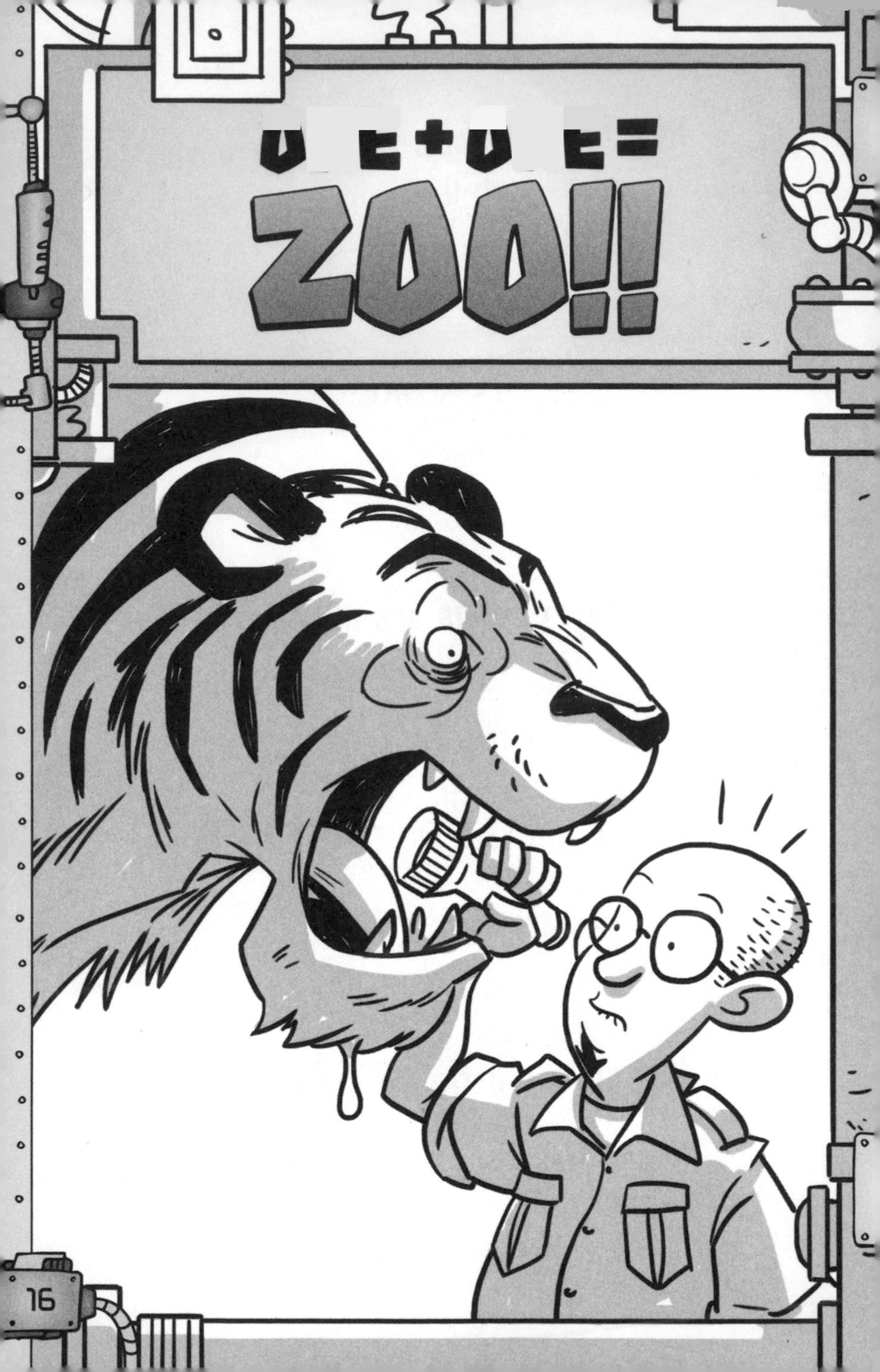
ZOO!!

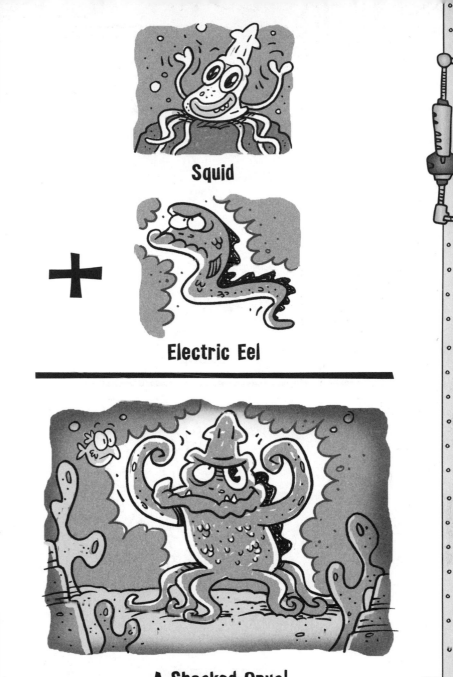

Squid

+

Electric Eel

A Shocked-Opus!

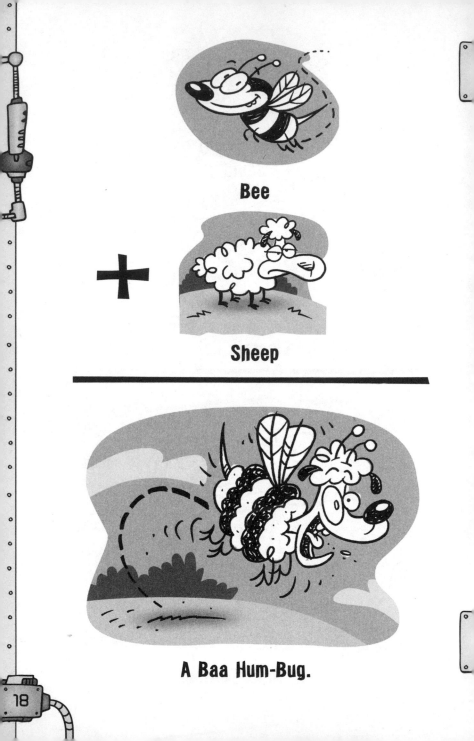

Bee

+

Sheep

A Baa Hum-Bug.

Cat

+

Lemon

A Sourpuss.

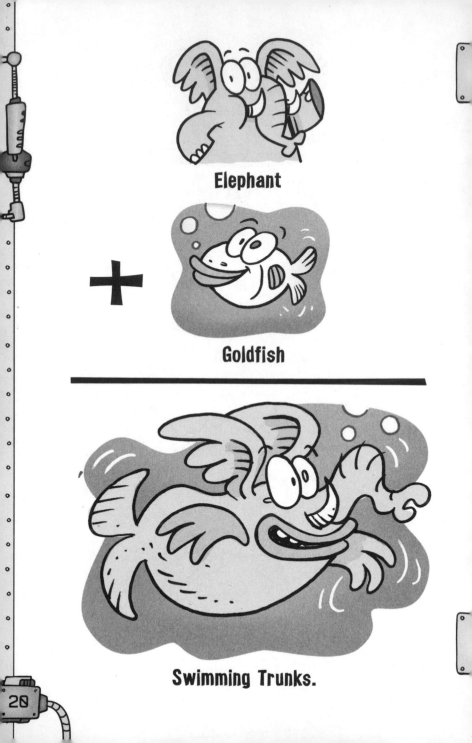

Elephant

+

Goldfish

Swimming Trunks.

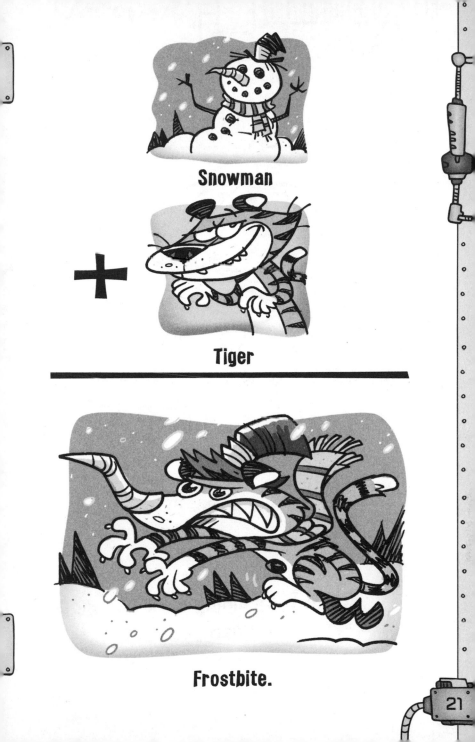

Snowman

+

Tiger

Frostbite.

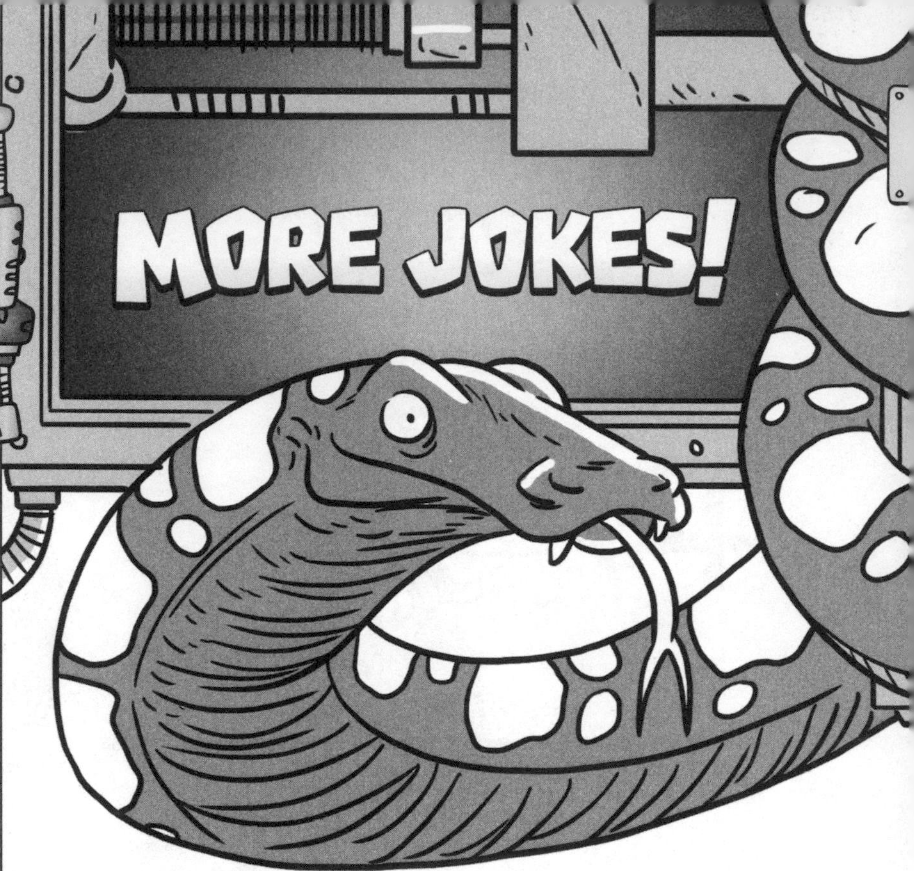
MORE JOKES!

Why did the fox cross the road?
To get to the chicken on the other side!

"Wow! It's raining cats and dogs!"
How can you tell?
"I just stepped in a poodle!"

Did you know the ancient Romans could talk to their pigs?

Really?

Yeah, they spoke Pig Latin.

What kind of animal goes "Oom, oom"?

A cow walking backward.

How do fleas move from one dog to another?

They itch hike.

Did you hear about the owl that lost its voice?

It didn't give a hoot.

What happened to the cat that swallowed a ball of yarn?

It had mittens!

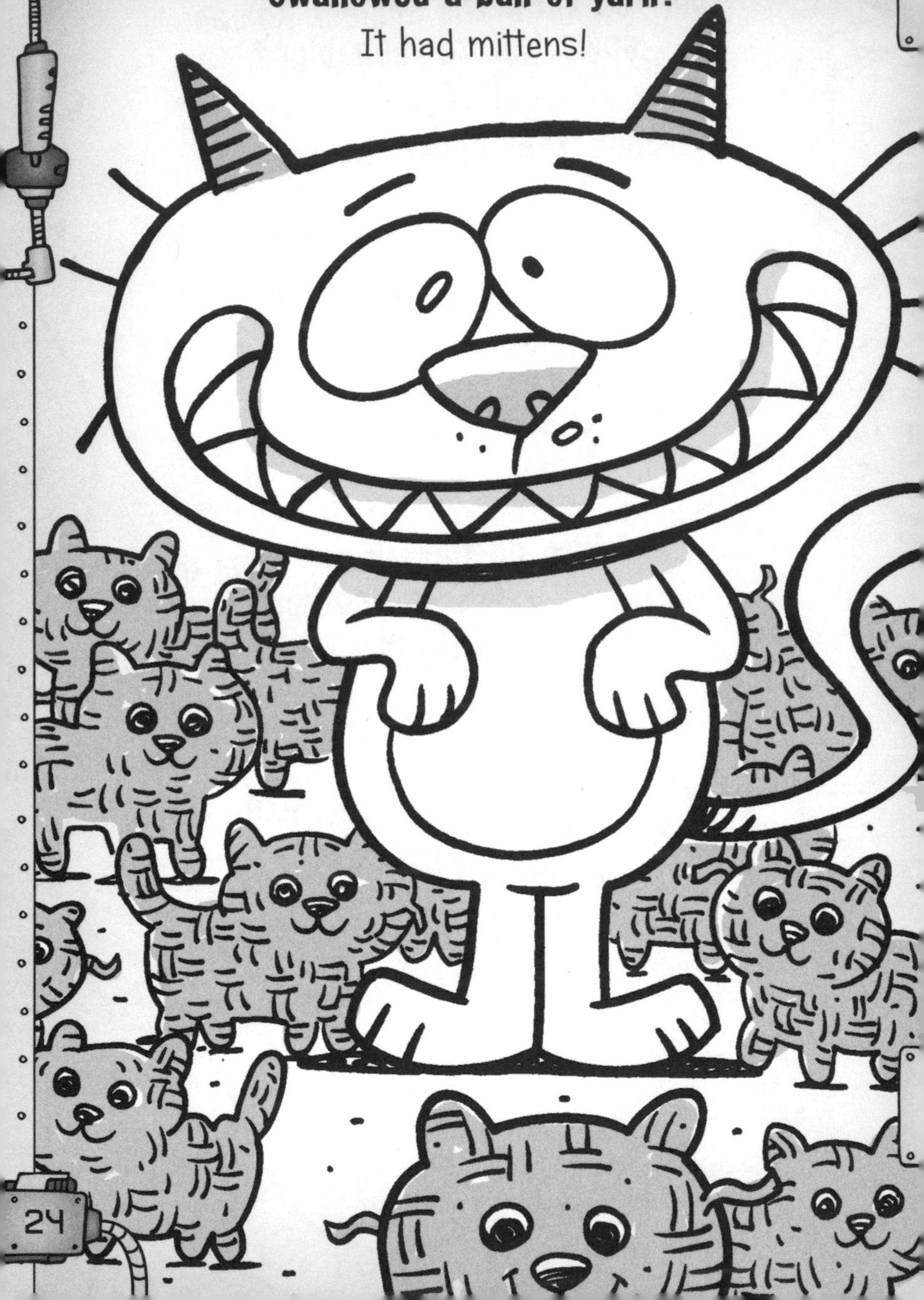

What did the mother buffalo say to her little boy when he went to school?

"Bison!"

What happens when a frog's car breaks down?

He has it toad.

Why do tigers have stripes?

So they aren't spotted.

Never play cards in the jungle. Why not?

There are too many cheetahs!

What do you call a crate full of ducks?
A box of quackers.

I heard your pet rabbit broke its leg!
Yes, he's very unhoppy.

Why can't Dalmatians hide from their owners?
Because they're always spotted.

Where do cows go on the weekends?
To the moovies.

Who stole the soap from the bathtub?
The robber ducky.

How do rabbits cross the ocean?
By hareplane.

Why do chickens make such bad basketball players?
They always fowl.

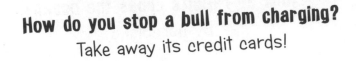

How do you stop a bull from charging?

Take away its credit cards!

What type of music do bunnies listen to?

Hip-hop.

What do you call a bird that's in pain?
An owwwwwwwwl!

How do you catch a unique animal?
Unique up on it.

What is an owl's favorite subject?
Owl-gebra!

What did the dog say about his day in the woods?
"Bark, bark, bark, bark, bark, bark . . . "

Why do baby skunks make the worst pets?
They're such little stinkers!

What is the biggest ant in the world?
An elephant.

What ant is good at math?
An accountant.

Why was the pony so quiet?
He was a little hoarse.

What do you give a bunny for dessert?
A hopsicle.

Why did the bunnies go on strike?

They wanted a raise in celery.

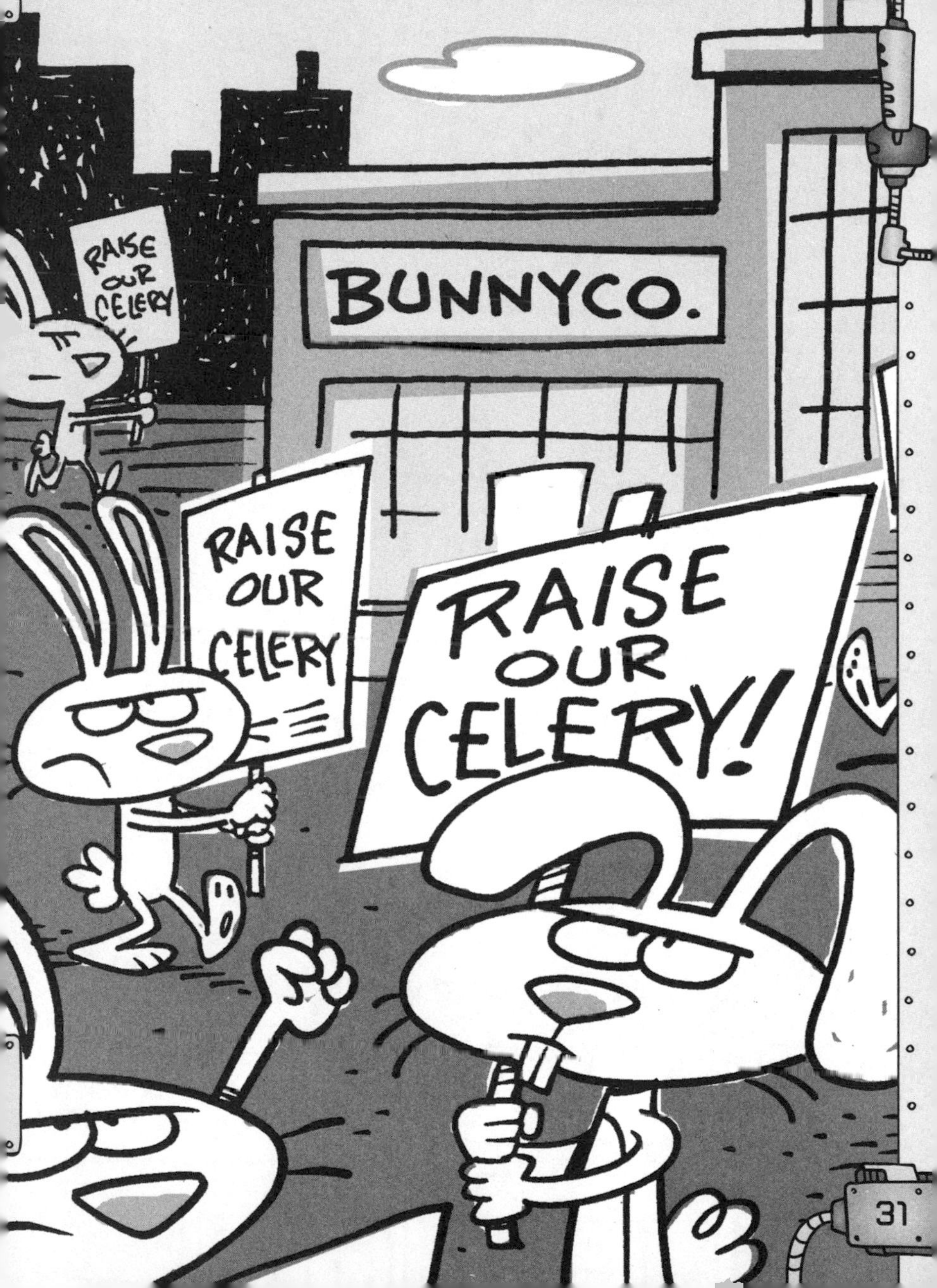
RAISE OUR CELERY
BUNNYCO.
RAISE OUR CELERY
RAISE OUR CELERY!

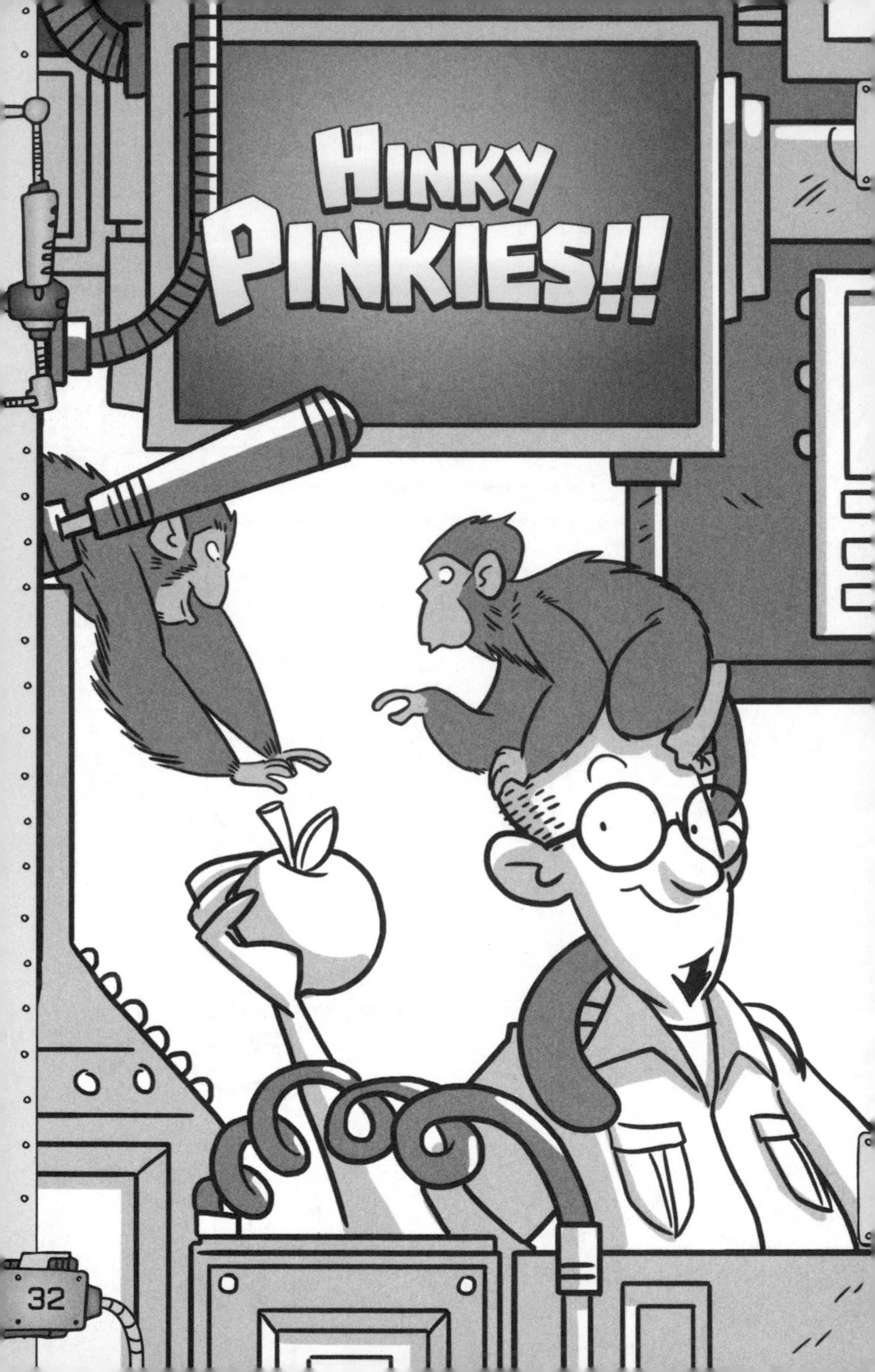
HINKY PINKIES!!

What do you call a
skinny little horse?

A BONY PONY

What kind of fruit do
gazelles like to eat?

ANTELOPE CANTELOUPE

What do monkeys use to travel through the air?

A BABOON BALLOON

What do you call a fruity drink for elks?

MOOSE JUICE

What do you get if you cross a gecko with a snowstorm?

A BLIZZARD LIZARD

What do you call your pet pooch when it's out in the rain?

A SOGGY DOGGY

What do you call a lamb that hates to spend money?

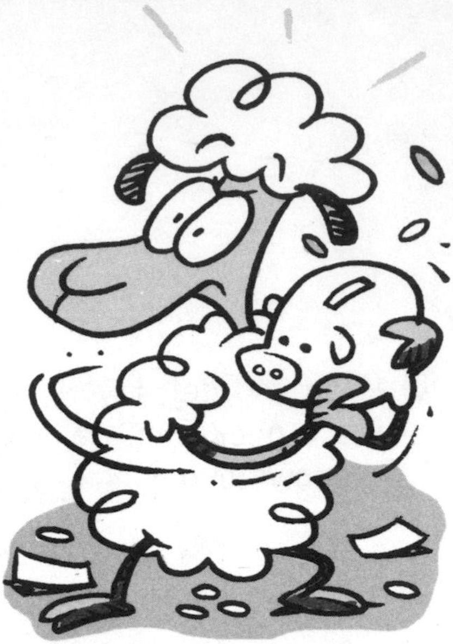

A CHEAP SHEEP

What do you get if you cross a centipede with a parrot?

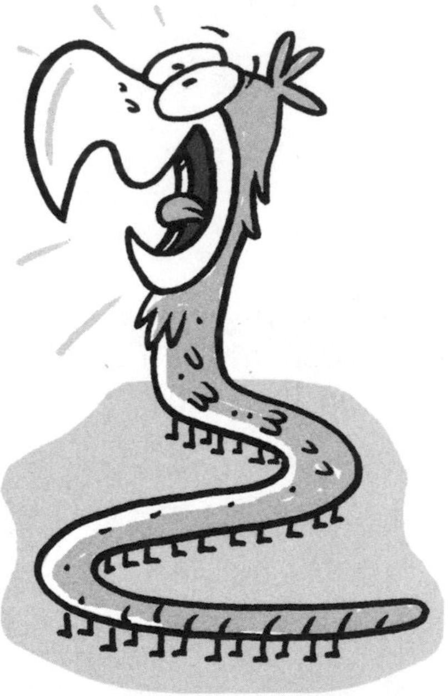

A WALKIE-TALKIE

What do you call a phony serpent?

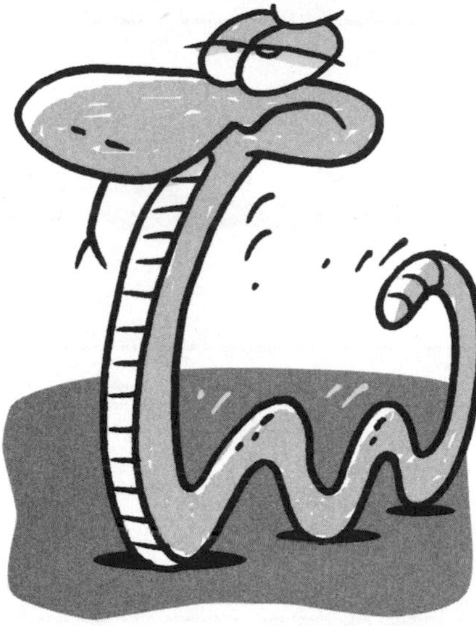

A FAKE SNAKE

What do you call a frog that vacations in Jamaica?

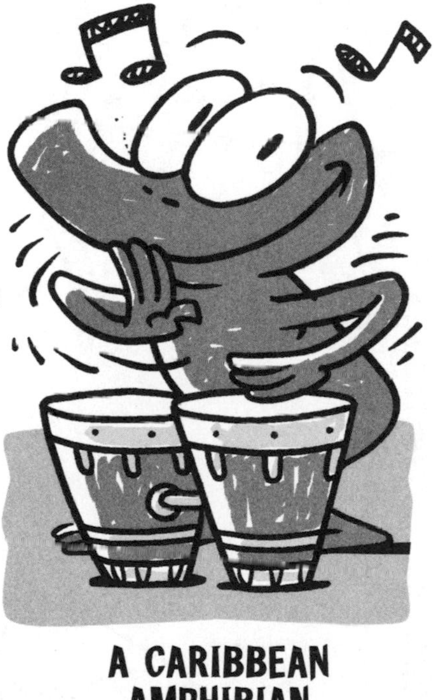

A CARIBBEAN AMPHIBIAN

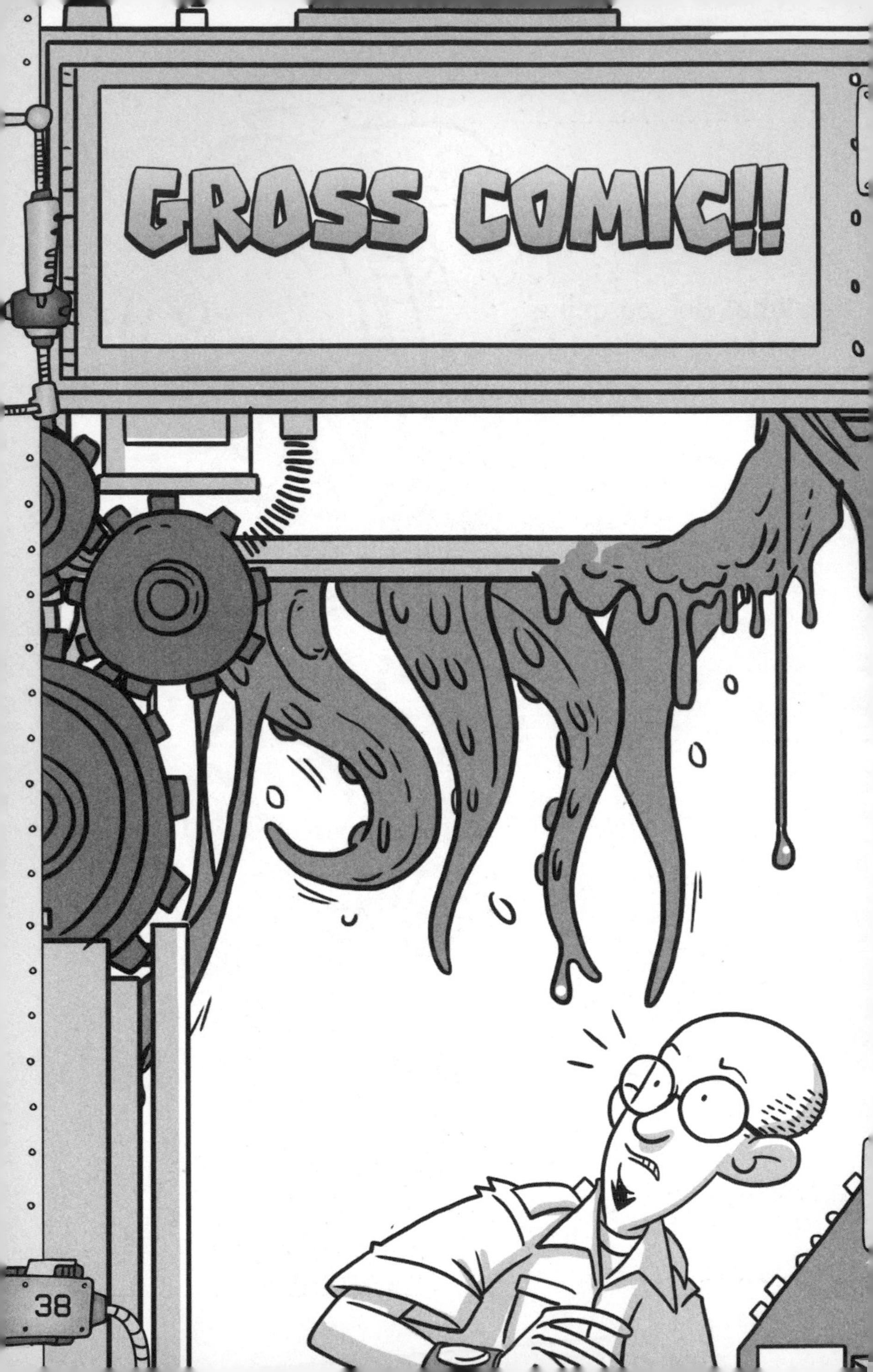
GROSS COMIC!!

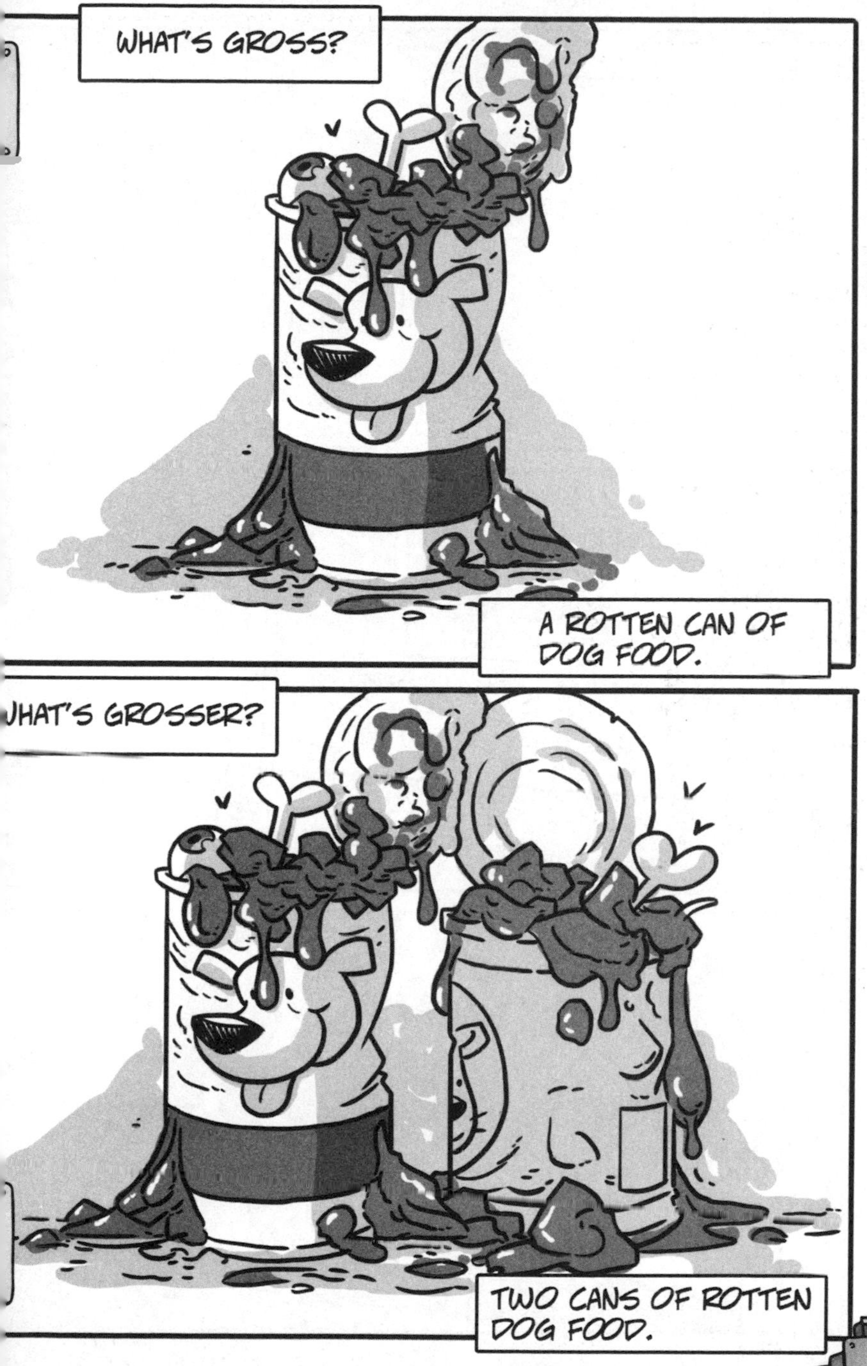
WHAT'S GROSS?
A ROTTEN CAN OF DOG FOOD.
WHAT'S GROSSER?
TWO CANS OF ROTTEN DOG FOOD.

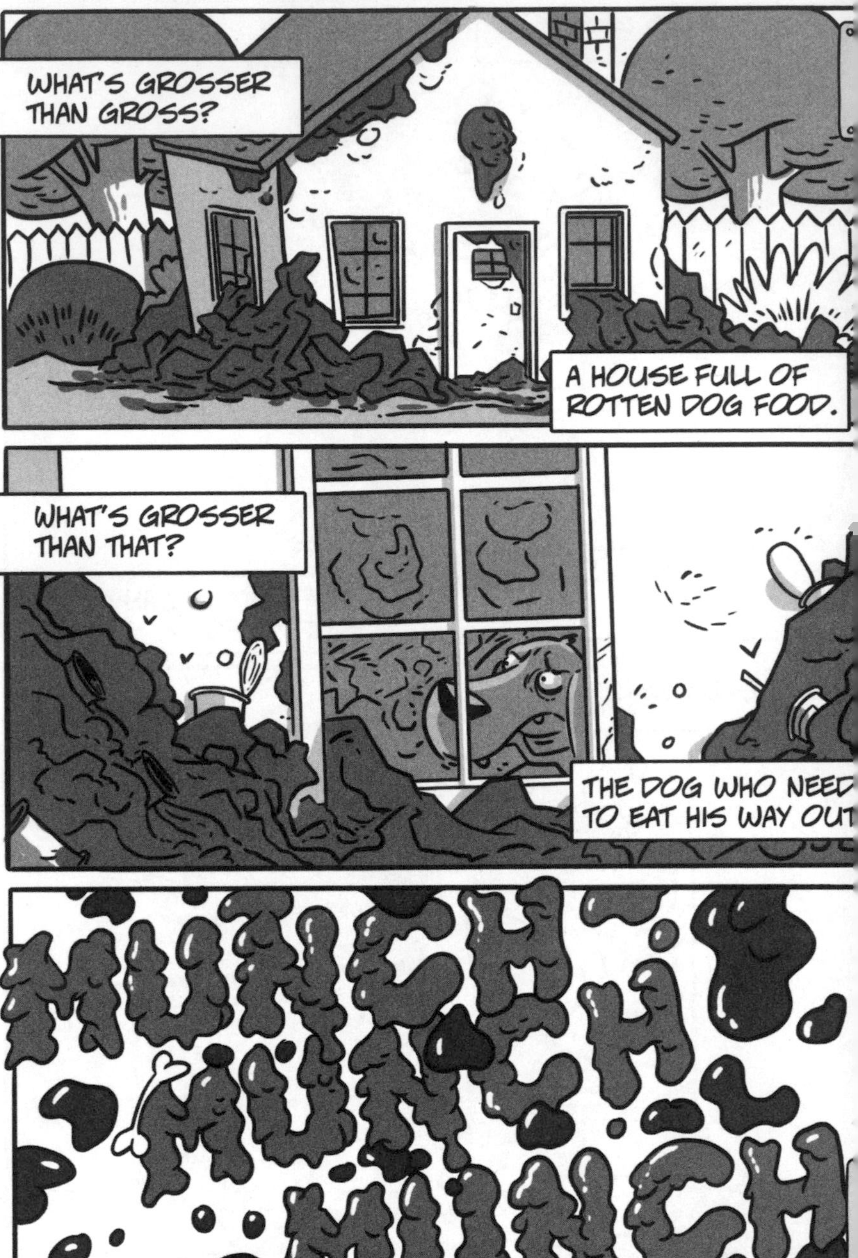
WHAT'S GROSSER THAN GROSS?
A HOUSE FULL OF ROTTEN DOG FOOD.
WHAT'S GROSSER THAN THAT?
THE DOG WHO NEED TO EAT HIS WAY OUT
MUNCH MUNCH MUNCH

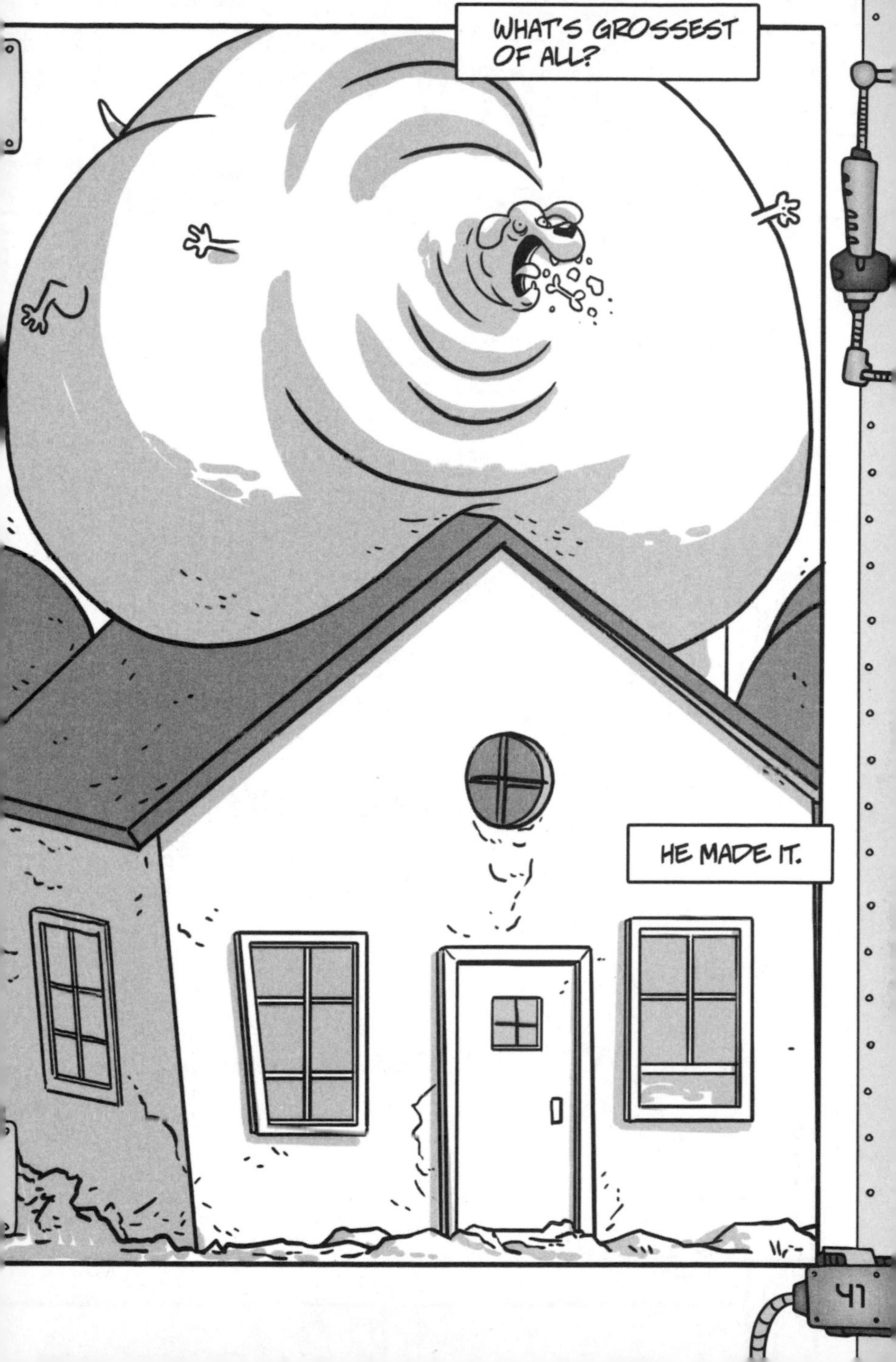
WHAT'S GROSSEST OF ALL?
HE MADE IT.

What's This? MORE JOKES!

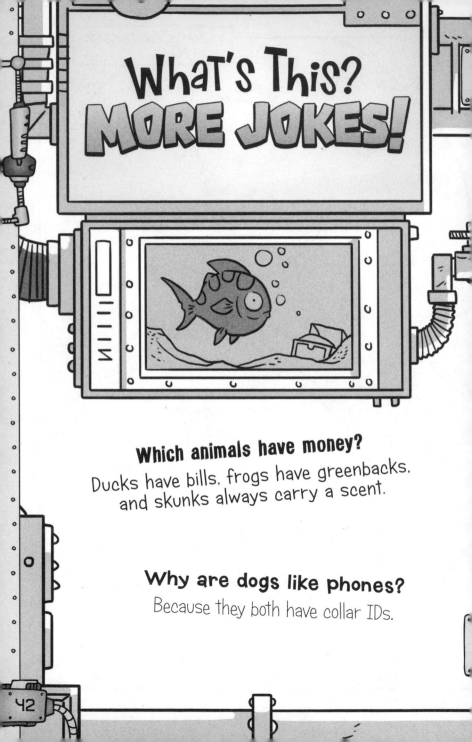

Which animals have money?

Ducks have bills, frogs have greenbacks, and skunks always carry a scent.

Why are dogs like phones?

Because they both have collar IDs.

What kind of dog likes to take bubble baths?
A sham-poodle.

**What did the cowboy say
when his dog ran away?**
"Doggone!"

How do lions like to start their day?
By catching up with the morning gnus!

Did you hear the joke about the skunk?
It stinks!

Have you ever seen a fishbowl?
No. How do they get their fins into those
holes in the balls?

Why was the little ant so confused?
Because all his uncles were aunts!

Never play basketball with porcupines.
They always make the most points!

Where do dogs hate to go shopping?
A flea market.

What's the worst part about hunting elephants?
Carrying the decoys!

What kind of pet can help you read?
An alphapet.

Why aren't elephants allowed on the beach?

Because sometimes they drop their trunks!

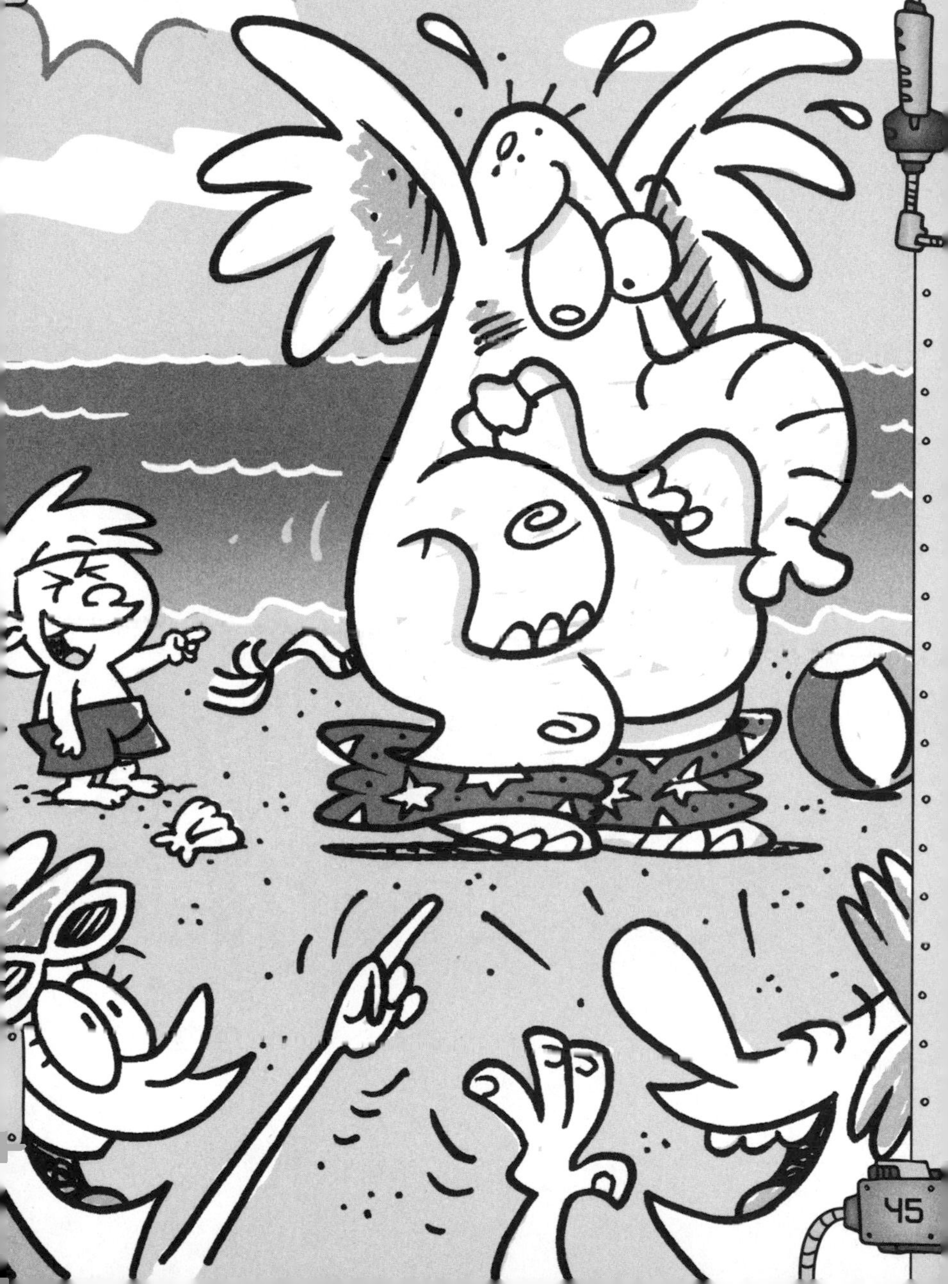

What kind of pet can you stand on?
A carpet.

Why did the girl oil her pet hamster?
Because it squeaked.

How did the fly get off the web?
It turned off the computer.

Why did the puppy bite the man's ankle?
Because it couldn't reach any higher.

**Know what a turkey is grateful
for on Thanksgiving?**
Vegetarians.

**What kind of pet can
you play in a band?**
A trumpet.

Why is a bee's hair always sticky?
Because it has a honeycomb.

What did one bee say to the other bee on a hot summer day?
"Swarm, isn't it?"

Why did the crow sit on the telephone wire?
He was making a long-distance caw.

How did the boy talk to his pet goldfish?
He dropped it a line.

Who did the seabird take on a date?
His gull friend.

What did the banana say when it saw the hungry monkey?
Nothing. The banana split!

Do rabbits use combs?
No, they use hare brushes.

Knock, knock.
Who's there?
Owl.
Owl who?
Owl tell you when you let me in!

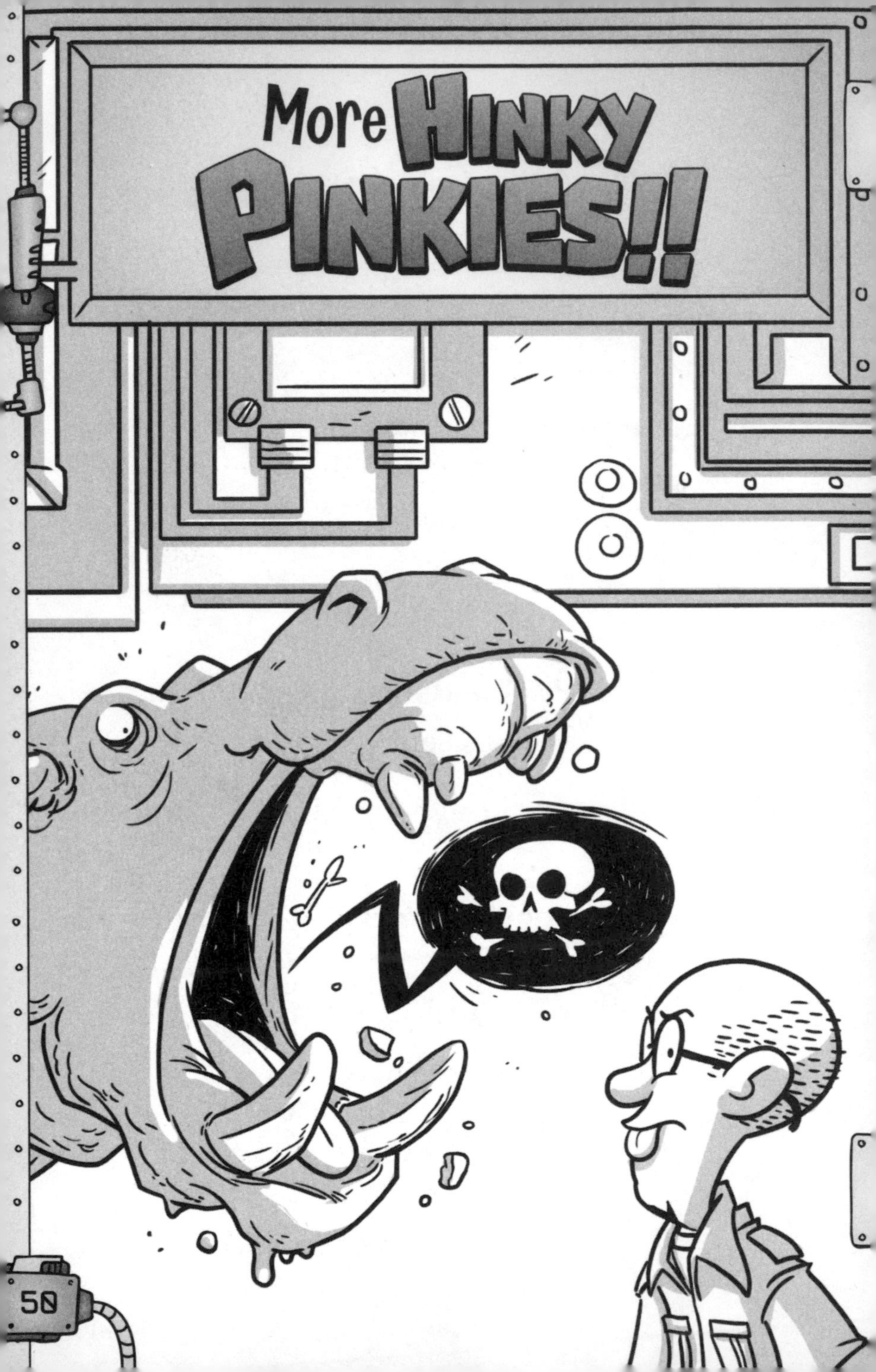
More HINKY PINKIES!!

What do you call a person who takes care of spotted cats?

A LEOPARD SHEPHERD

Where can you find orcas that break the law?

WHALE JAIL

What do you call a rabbit comedian?

A FUNNY BUNNY

What do you call the sound a lizard makes at the Grand Canyon?

A GECKO ECHO

What do you call a chameleon that can perform magic tricks?

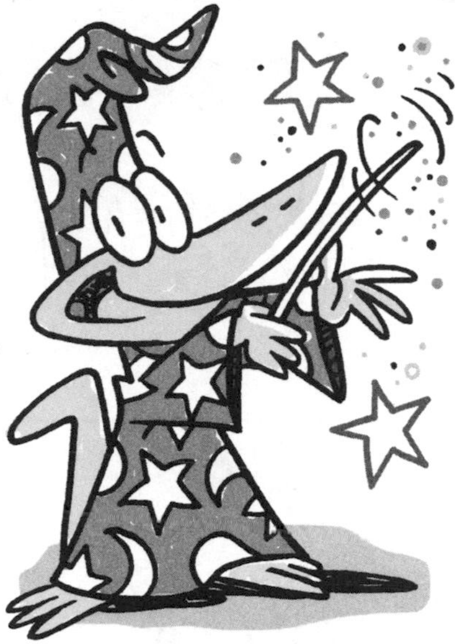

A LIZARD WIZARD

What do you call an overweight chimpanzee?

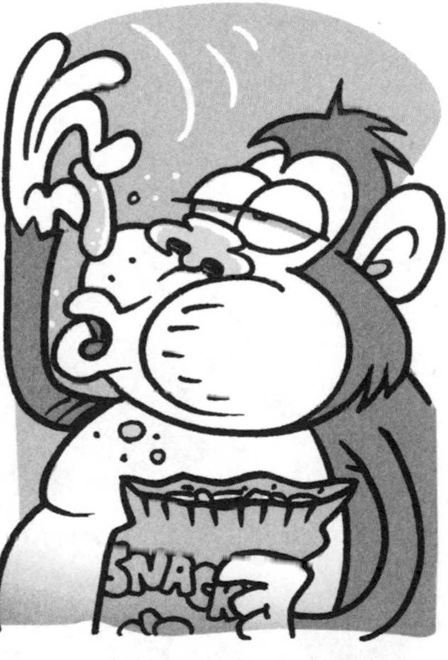
SNACK

A CHUNKY MONKEY

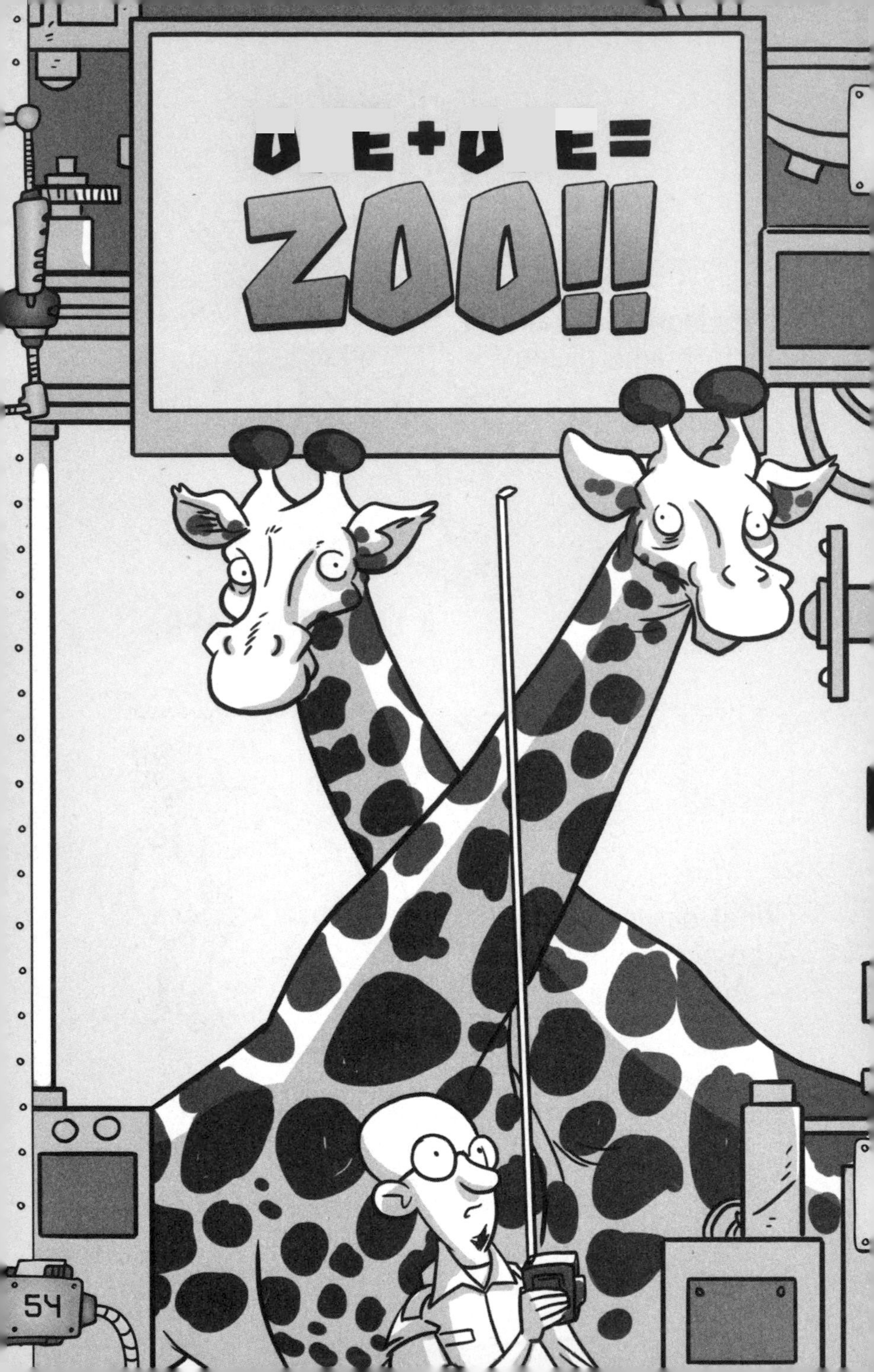
ZOO!!

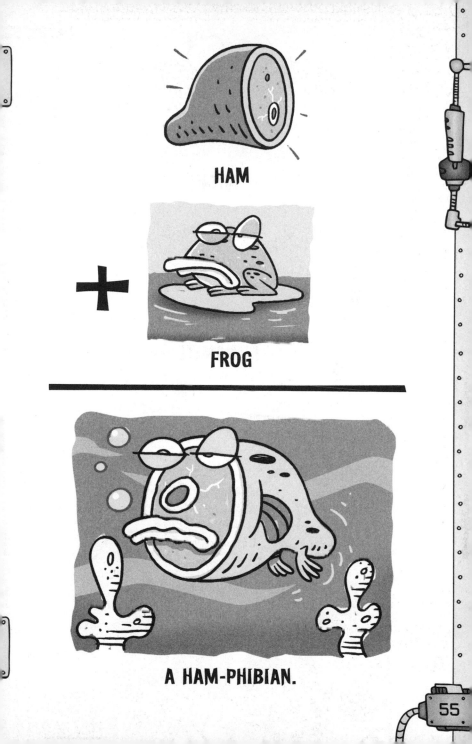

HAM

+

FROG

A HAM-PHIBIAN.

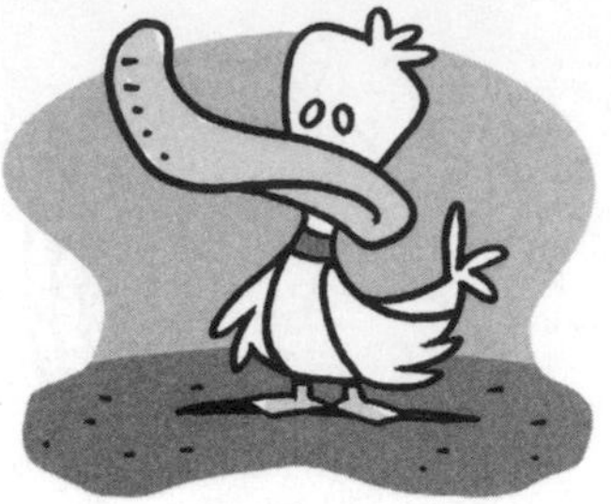

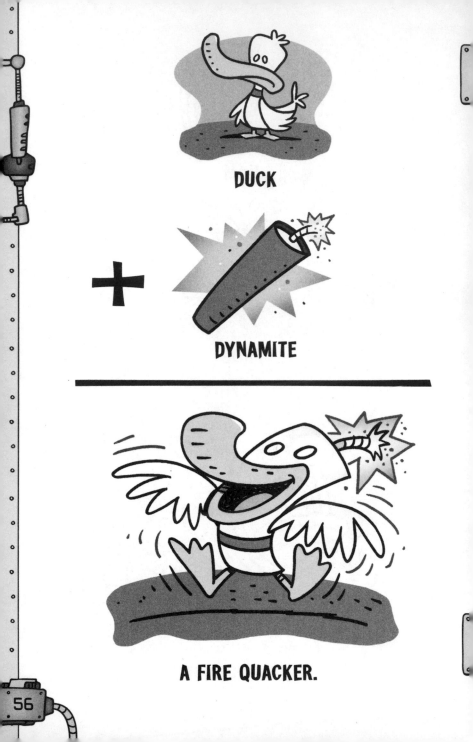

DUCK

+

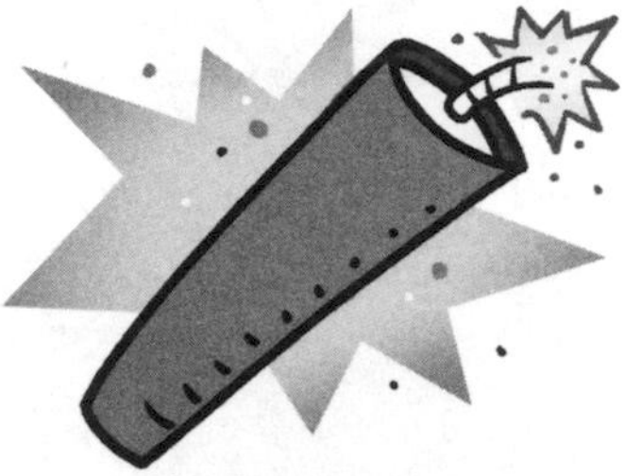

DYNAMITE

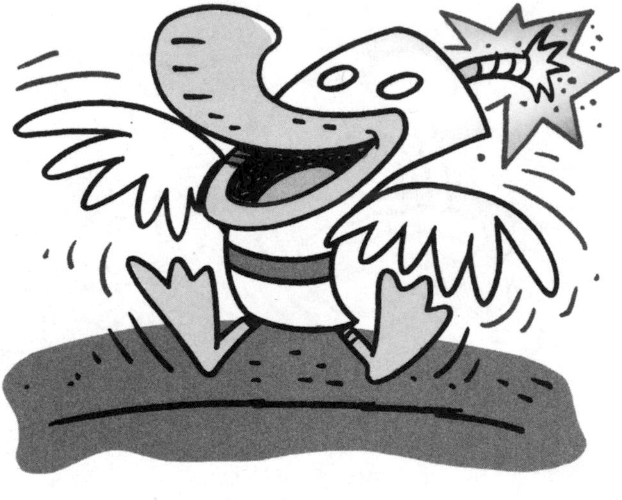

A FIRE QUACKER.

CAT

PARAKEET

SHREDDED TWEET.

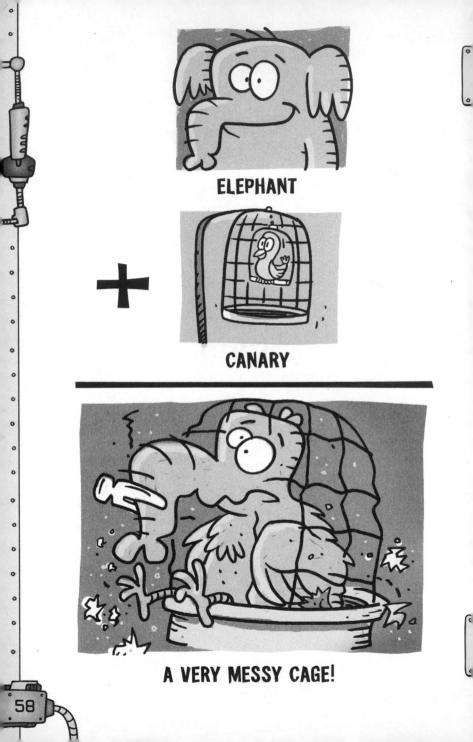

ELEPHANT

+

CANARY

A VERY MESSY CAGE!

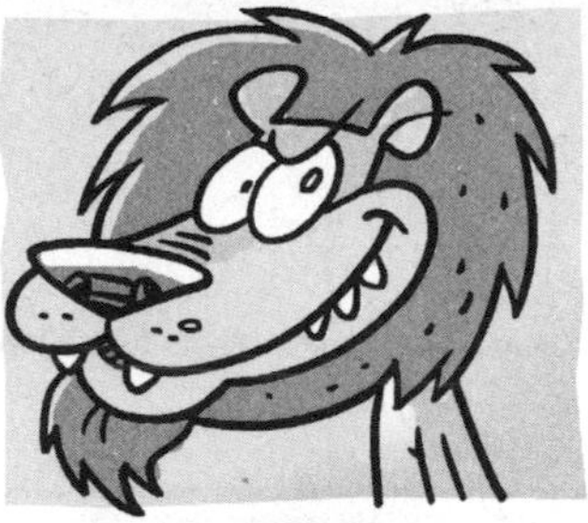

LION

+

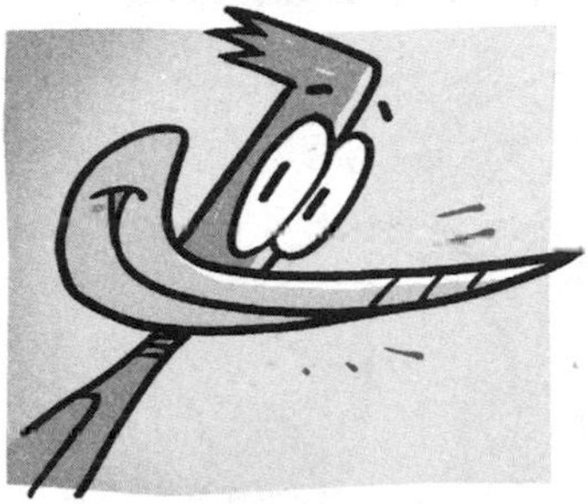

WOODPECKER

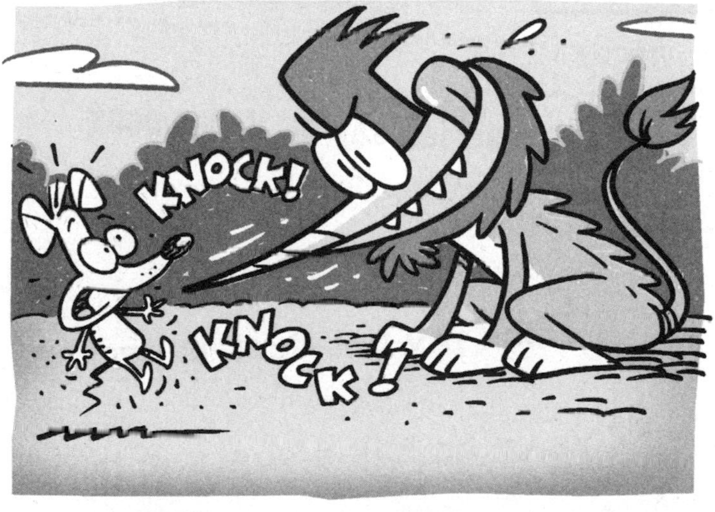
KNOCK!
KNOCK!

AN ANIMAL THAT KNOCKS BEFORE IT EATS YOU.

This MUST be some kind of joke!
MORE JOKES?!

What do canaries say on Halloween?
"Trick or tweet!"

I think my pet duck is broken.
Broken?
Yeah, he has a quack in him.

What is cat fur?
Fur chasing mice!

Why do seagulls fly over the sea?
Because if they flew over the bay, they'd be bagels?

What kind of dog cheers at a football game?
A Pom-Pomeranian

Why did the fried chicken cross the road?

Because she saw a fork up ahead!

How do you fix a broken gorilla?

Use a monkey wrench.

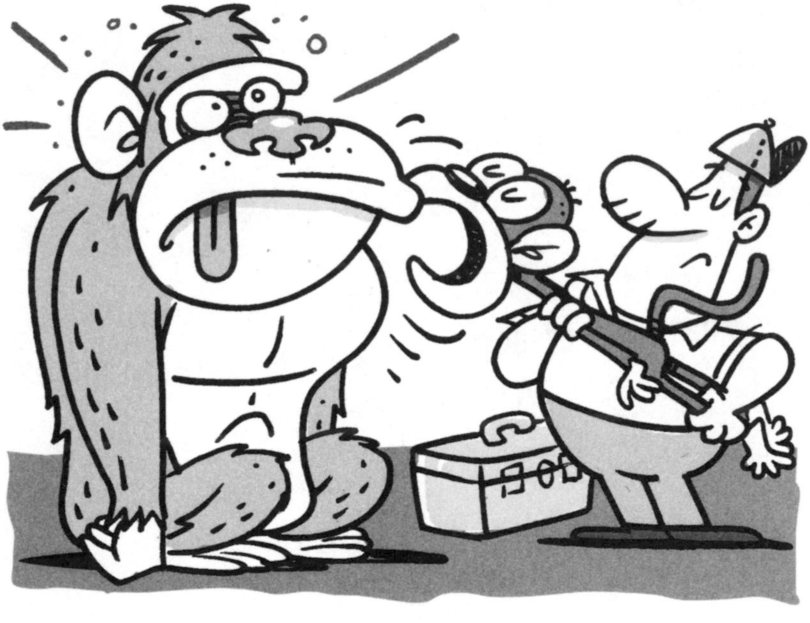
TOOLS

What do you say to a hitch-hiking kangaroo?
"Hop in!"

**Did you know it takes three sheep
to make one sweater?**
Wow! I didn't even know they could knit!

**Did you hear about the lobster
that bought a new car?**
It was a crustacean-wagon.

Why do birds fly south for the winter?
It's too far to walk.

What game do little mice like to play?
Hide and squeak.

What do frogs wear on their feet?
Open toad shoes.

Where do you send a sick pony?
To the horse-pital.

How do you get down off an elephant?
You don't get down off an elephant! You get down off a duck.

How do you measure a dog's temperature?
By pedigrees.

What do whales like to chew for a snack?
Blubber gum.

What does a 400-pound canary say?

"Here, kitty, kitty, kitty!"

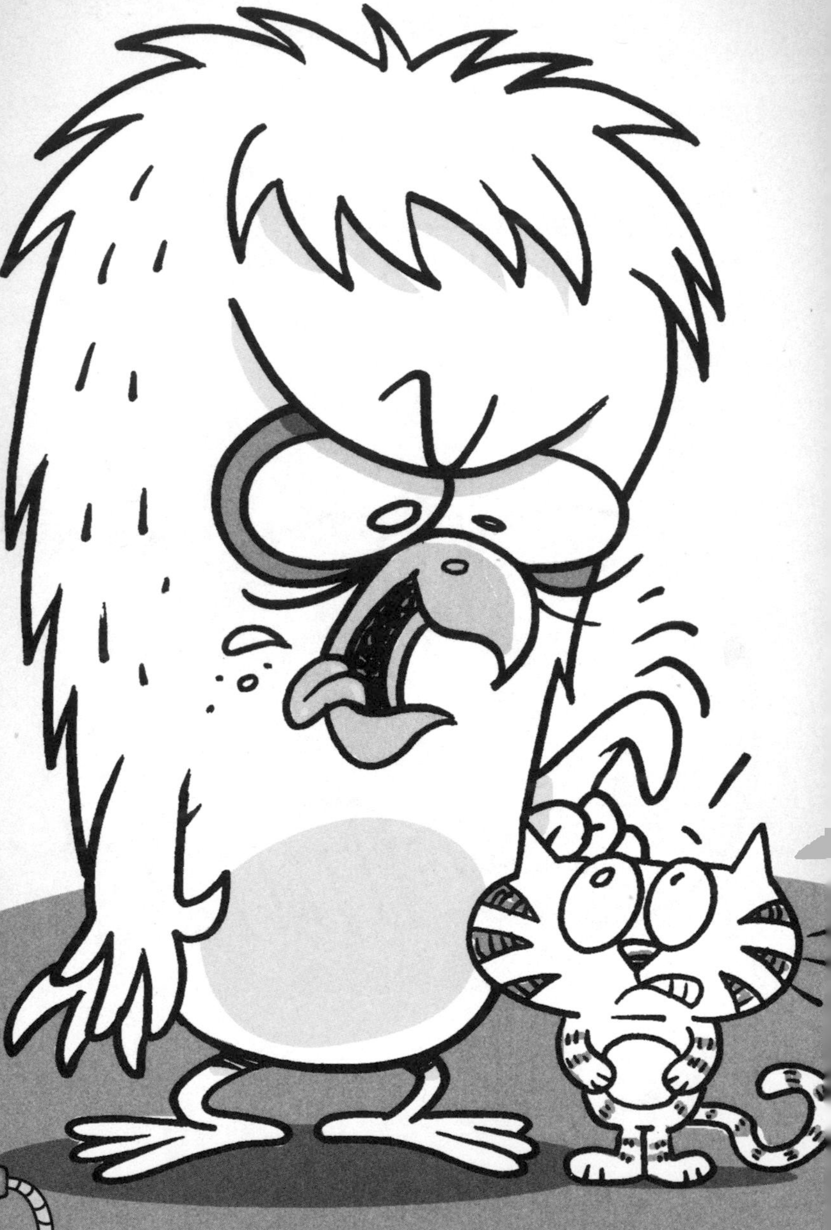

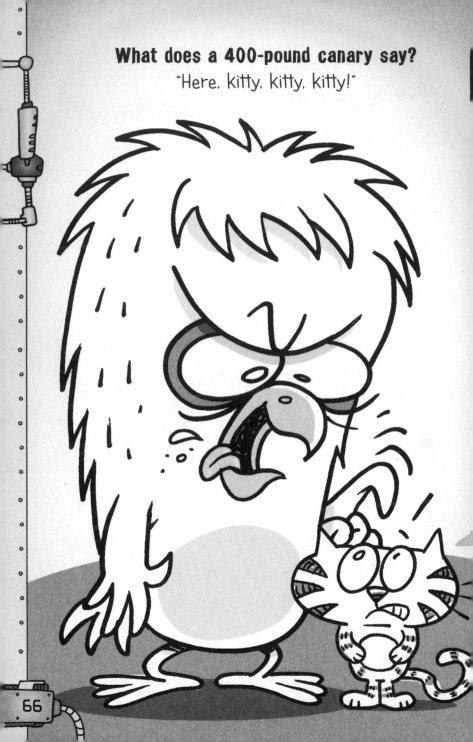

What do you call a basketball player's pet chicken?
A personal fowl.

Why do they put bells on cows?
Because their horns don't work.

Why did the teacher excuse the firefly from class?
Because it really had to glow!

Did you hear that a skunk wrote a book?
It became a best-smeller.

Can an elephant jump higher than a house?
Of course it can. Houses can't jump at all.

What did the little mouse say when it saw a bat for the first time?
"Look! An angel!"

What's big and gray and doesn't matter?
An irrelephant.

What happened when the dog performed with the flea circus?

He stole the show!

What did the bee say to the flower?

"Hey, bud, when do you open?"

HUNTER #1:

"Hey, I thought you were going bear hunting."

HUNTER #2:

"I was. But then I saw a sign on the highway that said 'Bear Left' so I came home."

Why was the rabbit so upset?
He was having a bad hare day!

What do you call a dumb bunny?
A hare brain!

Which part of a fish weighs the most?
The scales!

Why don't oysters share their pearls?
Because they're shellfish!

What's an elephant's favorite vegetable?
Squash.

**What do you call an owl
with a deep voice?**
A growl.

Why are elephants so poor?
They work for peanuts.

**What is a snake's
favorite dance?**
The mamba.

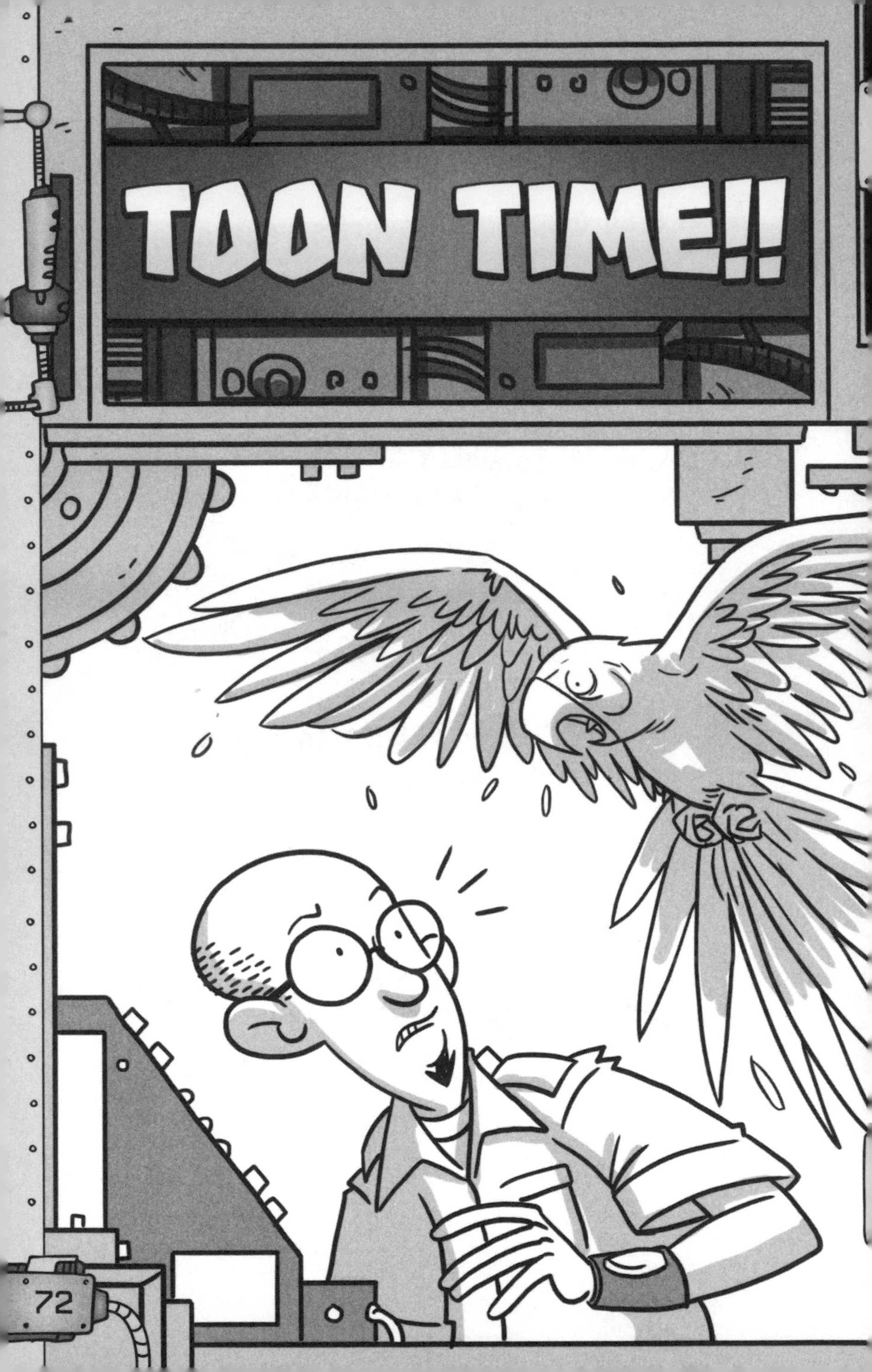
TOON TIME!!
72

"I THINK SHE'S BEEN TAKING STEROIDS."

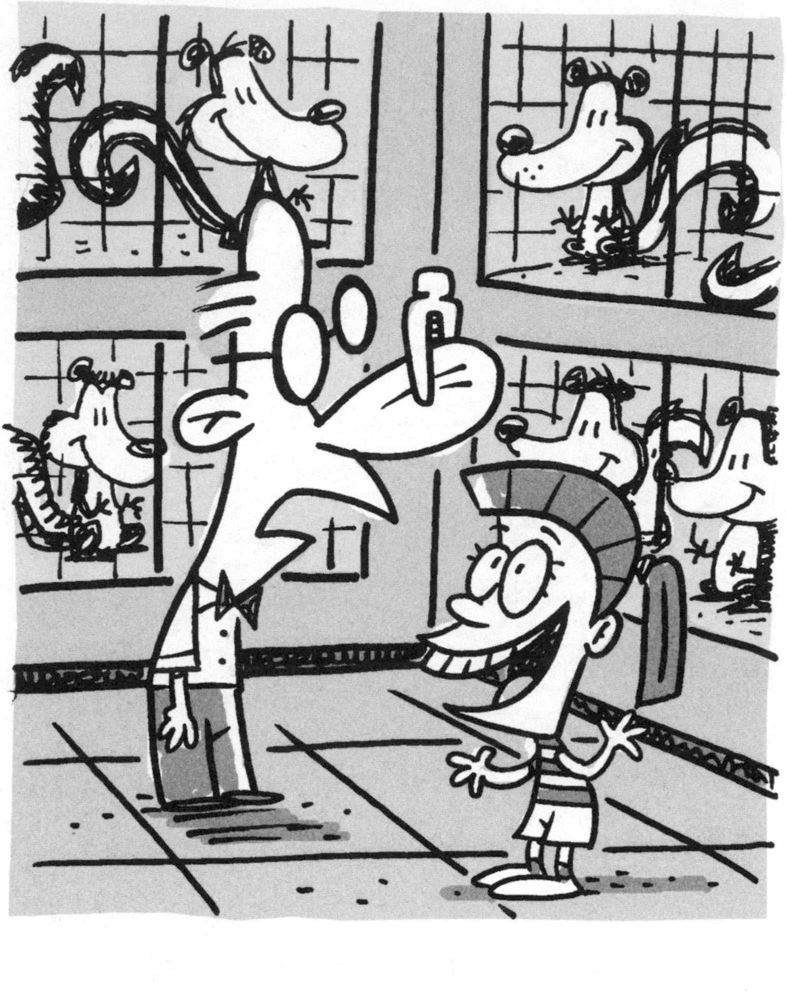

KID: "Do you have any pet skunks?"

PET SHOP OWNER: "Yes, quite a phew!"

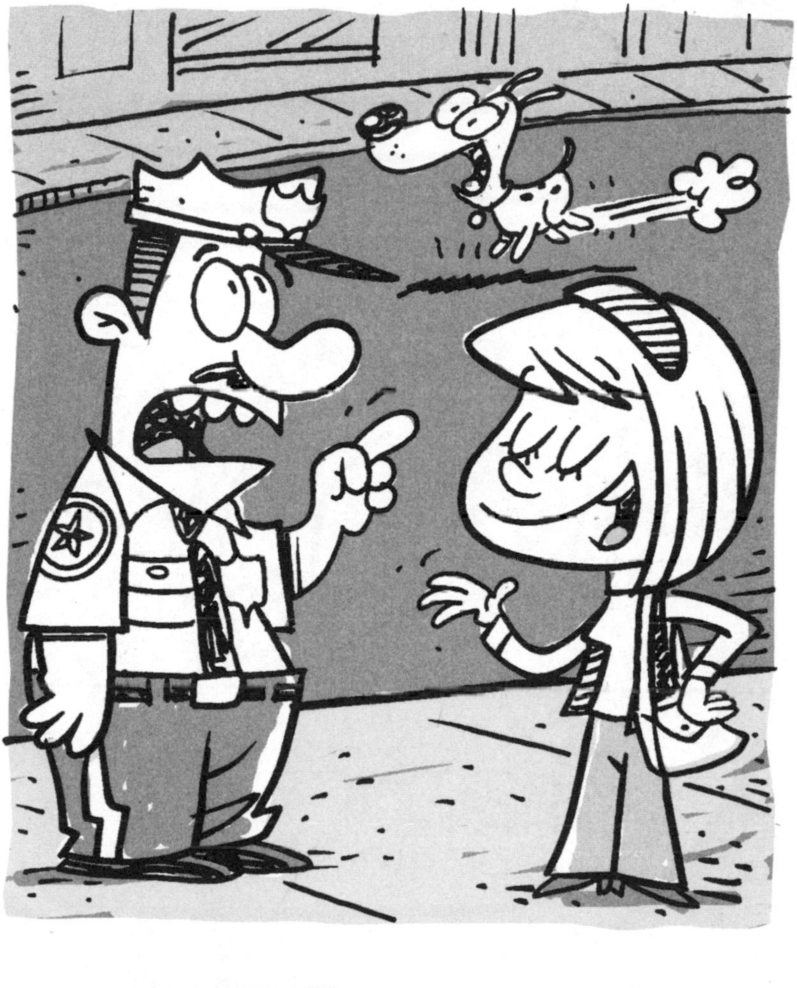

POLICE OFFICER: "Young woman, what is your dog doing in the street?"

GIRL: "Seven miles an hour."

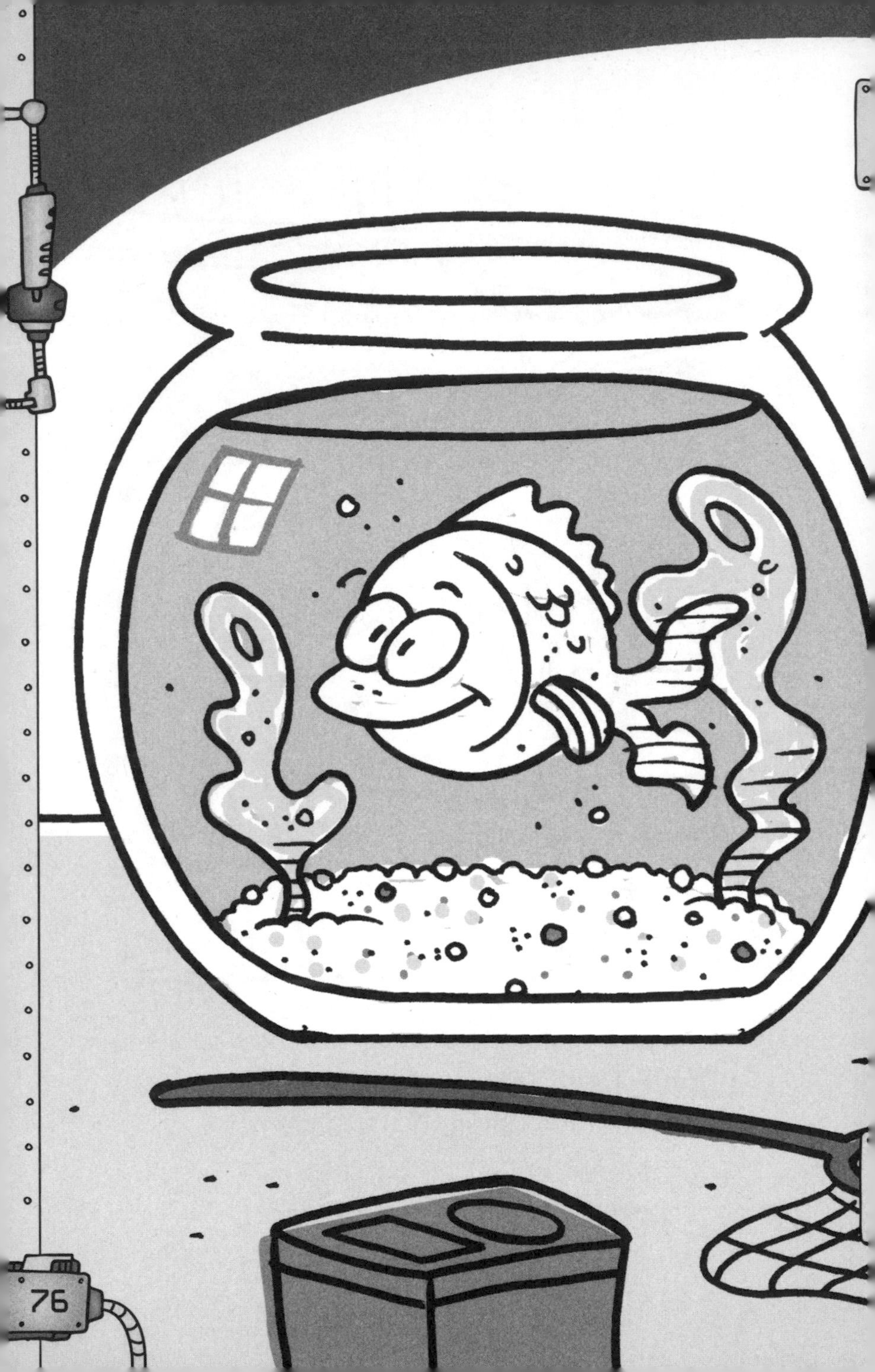
76

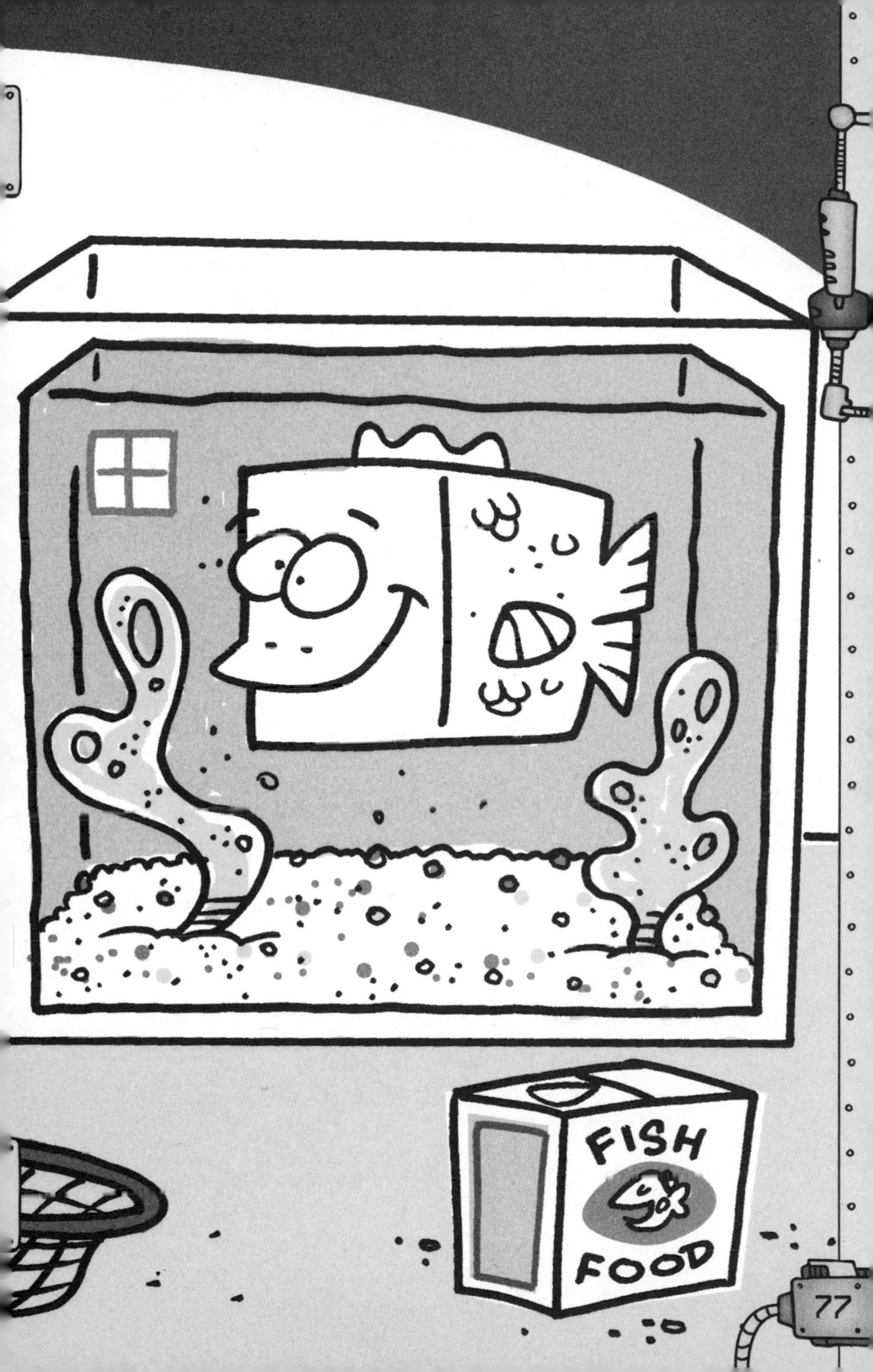
FISH
FOOD

FLippin' OUT!

Kanga-rude!

1. Grab the bottom-right corner of page 79.

2. Flip page 79 back and forth without letting go.

3. Keep an eye on page 81.

4. If you flip fast enough, pages 79 and 81 will look like one, animated picture!

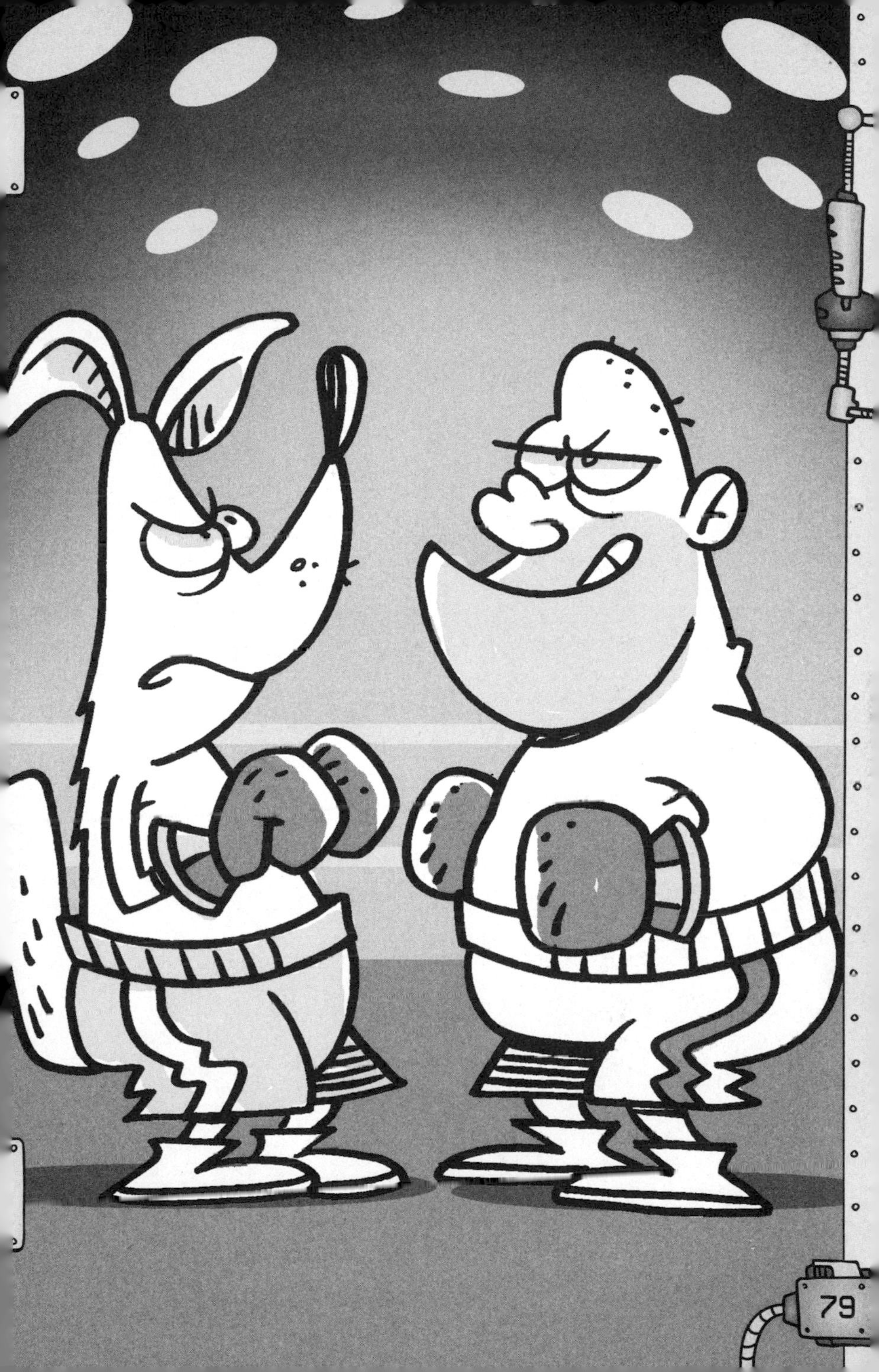

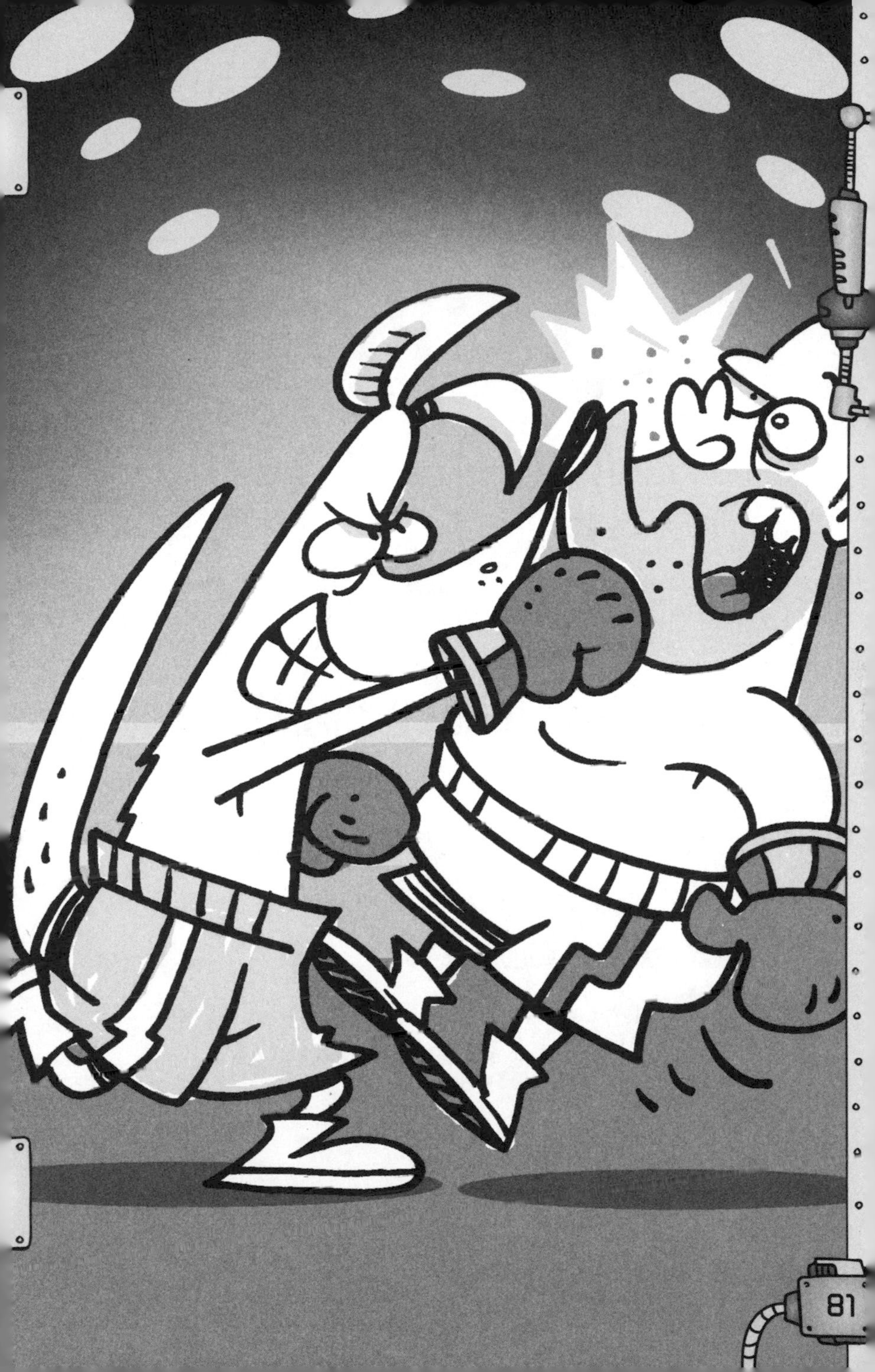

FLippin' OUT!

Lickety-split!

1. Grab the bottom-right corner of page 83.

2. Flip page 83 back and forth without letting go.

3. Keep an eye on page 85.

4. If you flip fast enough, pages 83 and 85 will look like one, animated picture!

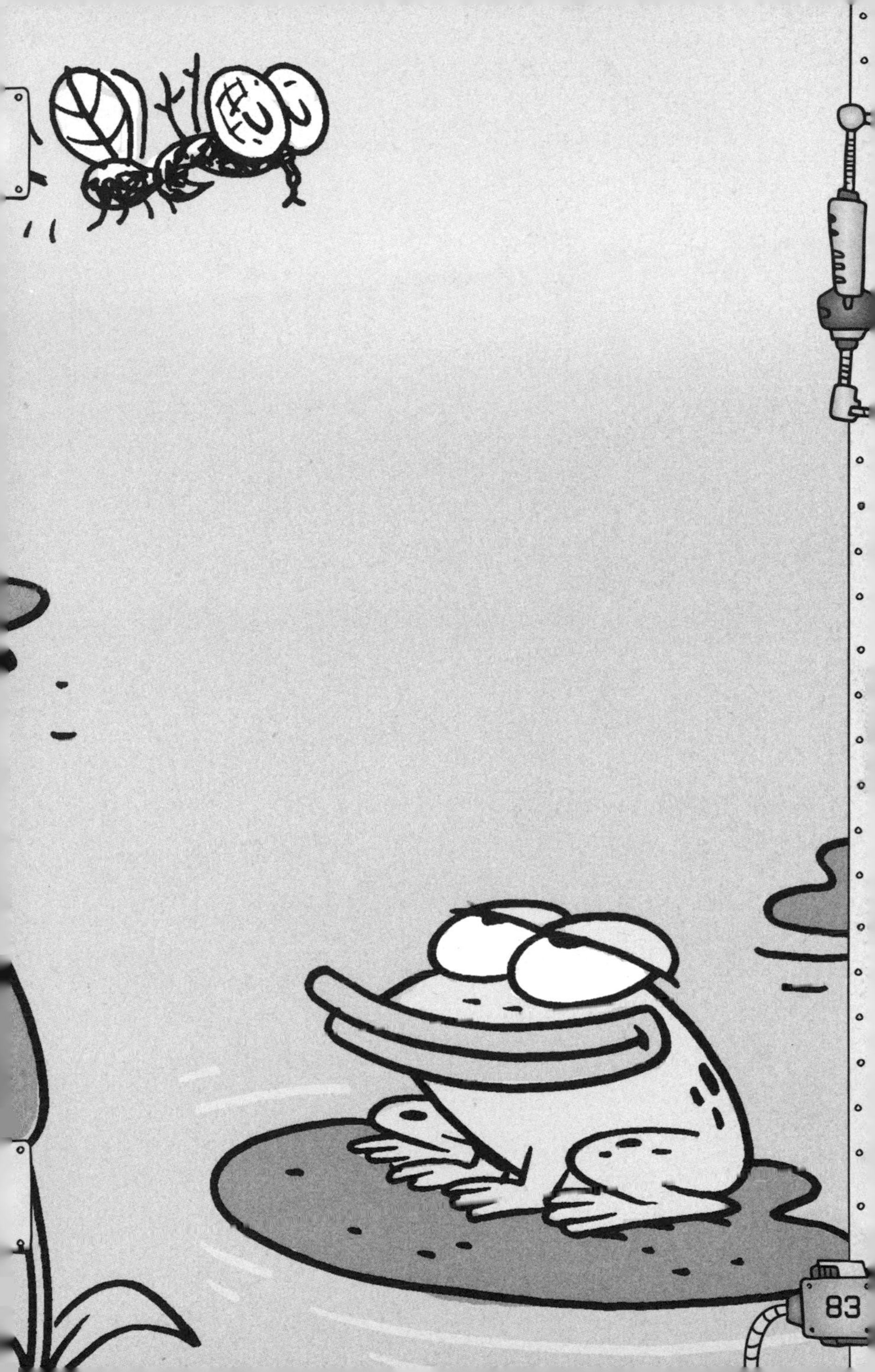

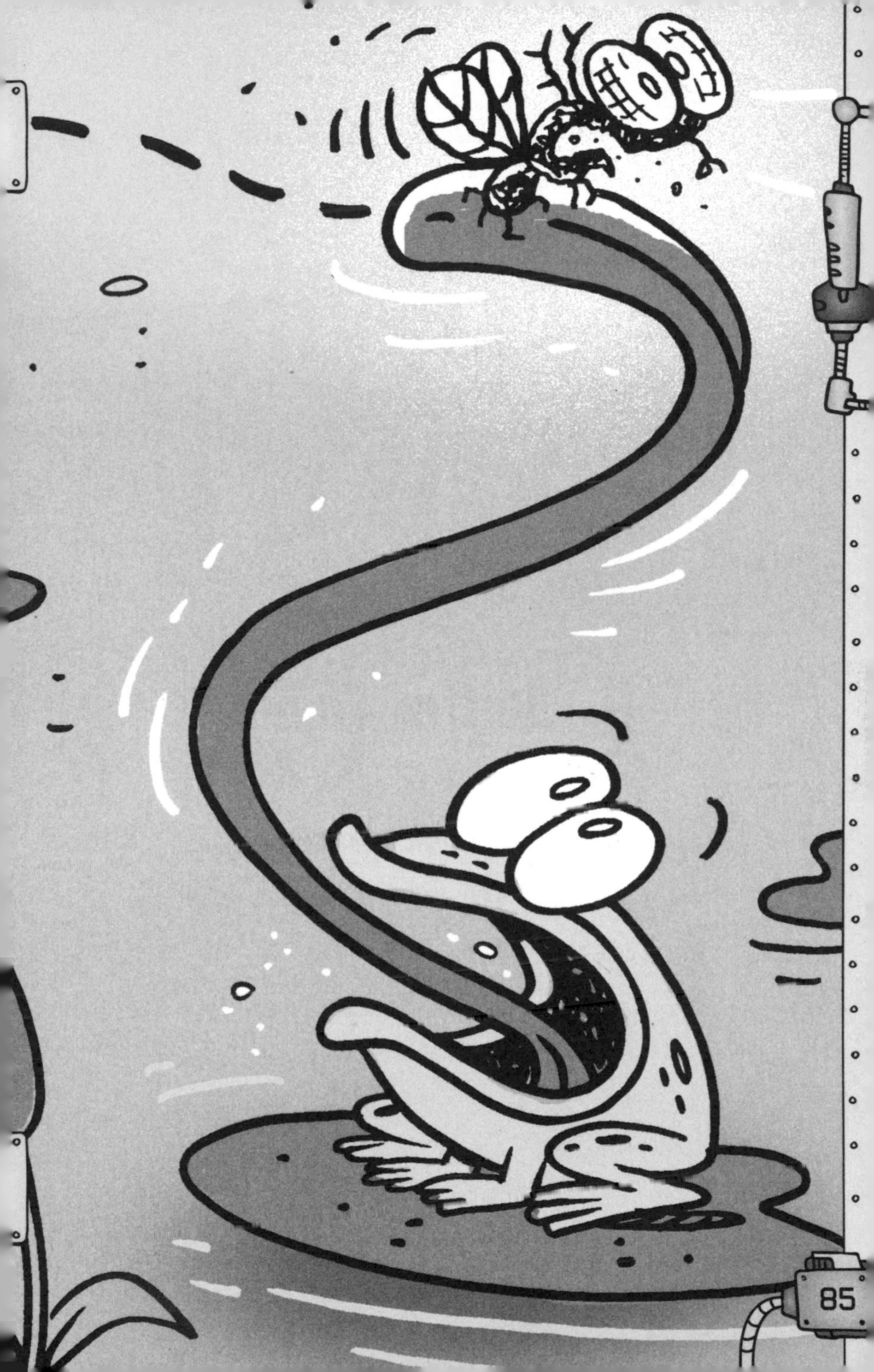

Flippin' OUT!

Puffer Fish!

1. Grab the bottom-right corner of page 87.

2. Flip page 87 back and forth without letting go.

3. Keep an eye on page 89.

4. If you flip fast enough, pages 87 and 89 will look like one, animated picture!

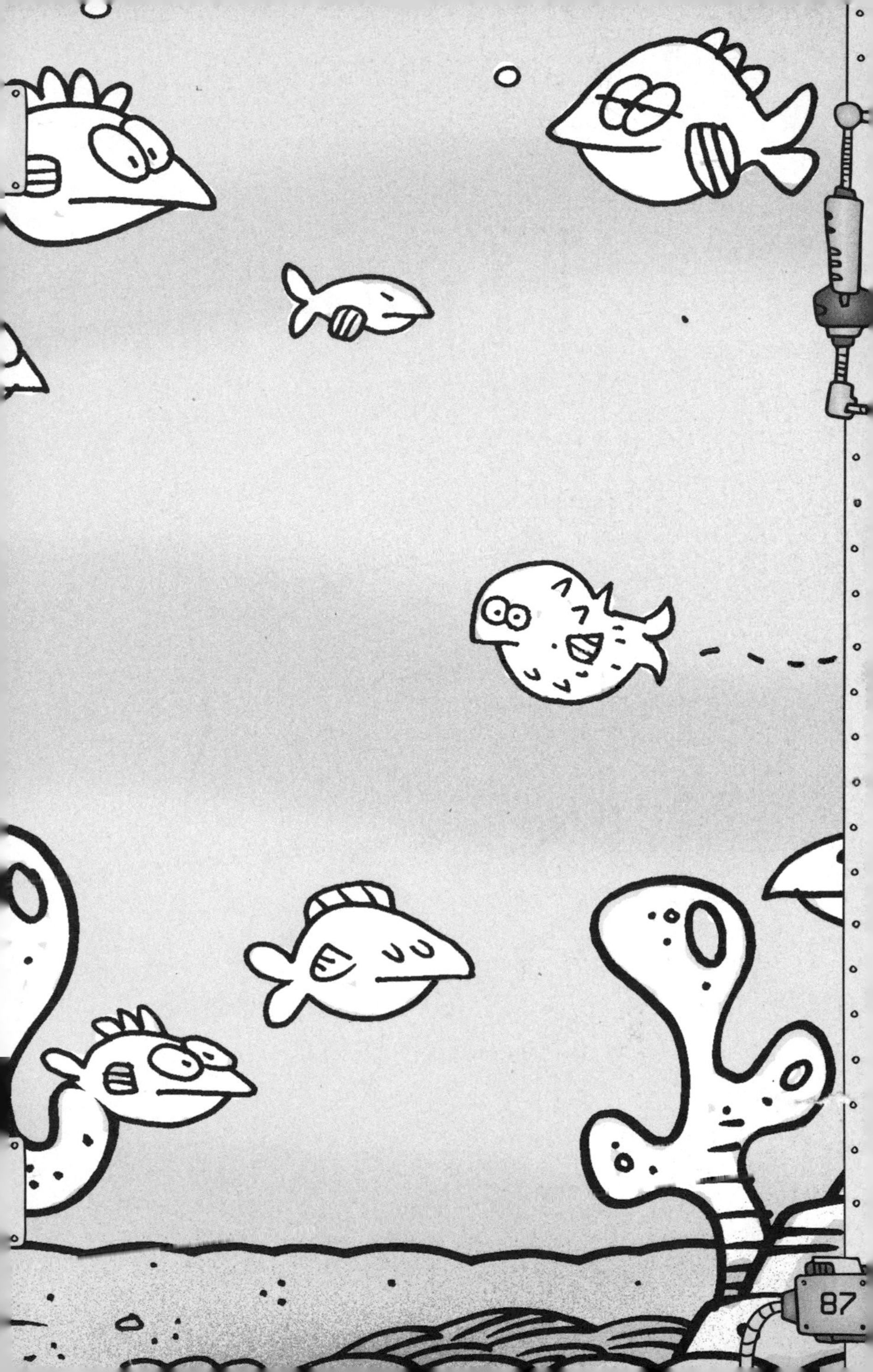

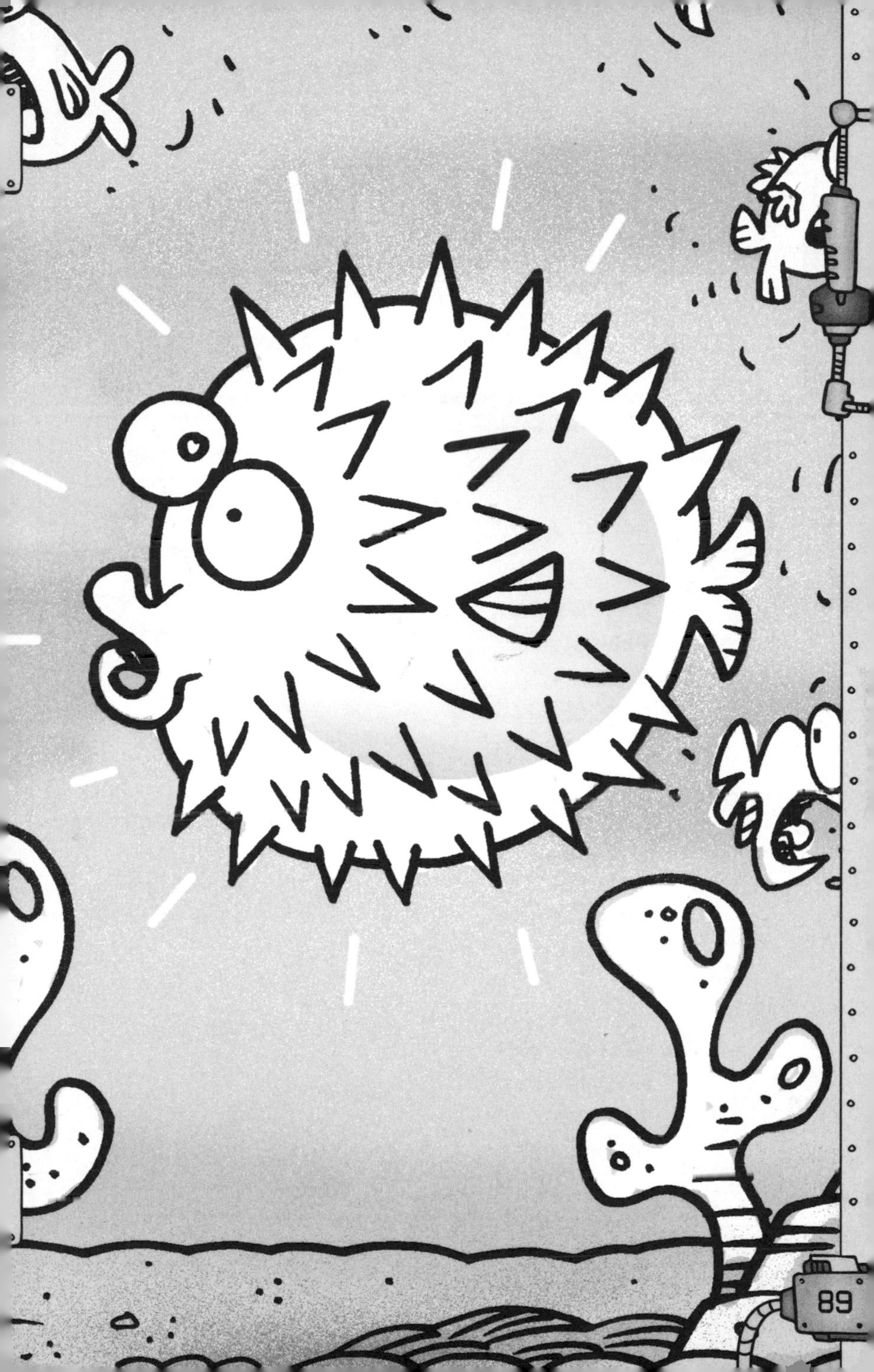

How to Draw

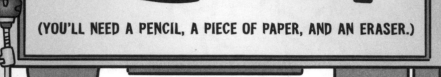

A BEAR!

(YOU'LL NEED A PENCIL, A PIECE OF PAPER, AND AN ERASER.)

1. USING YOUR PENCIL, DRAW A CIRCLE ON YOUR PAPER. THEN DRAW TWO LINES THROUGH THE CIRCLE, AS SHOWN AT RIGHT.

2. ADD A LARGE, ROUND NOSE TO YOUR BEAR'S HEAD.

3. NEXT, DRAW TWO SMALL CIRCLES FOR EYEBALLS. MAKE SURE THE EYES LINE UP ON THE CENTER LINE. DON'T FORGET THE PUPILS!

4. THEN GIVE YOUR BEAR TWO EARS. MAKE THEM BIG ENOUGH FOR HIM TO HEAR!

5. ERASE THE TWO LINES FROM STEP #1. THEN ADD DETAILS TO YOUR BEAR! GROWL!

AUTHOR

MICHAEL DAHL

HAS WRITTEN MORE THAN 200 BOOKS FOR YOUNG READERS. HE IS THE AUTHOR OF THE SUPER-FUNNY JOKE BOOKS SERIES, ***THE EVERYTHING KIDS' JOKE BOOKS,*** THE SCINTILLATING ***DUCK GOES POTTY,*** AND TWO HUMOROUS MYSTERY SERIES: FINNEGAN ZWAKE (A "WISECRACKING RIOT" ACCORDING TO THE ***CHICAGO TRIBUNE***) AND HOCUS POCUS HOTEL. HE TOURED THE COUNTRY WITH AN IMPROV TROUPE, AND BEGAN HIS AUSPICIOUS COMIC CAREER IN 5TH GRADE WHEN HIS STAND-UP ROUTINE MADE HIS MUSIC TEACHER LAUGH SO HARD SHE FELL OFF HER CHAIR. SHE IS NOT AVAILABLE FOR COMMENT.

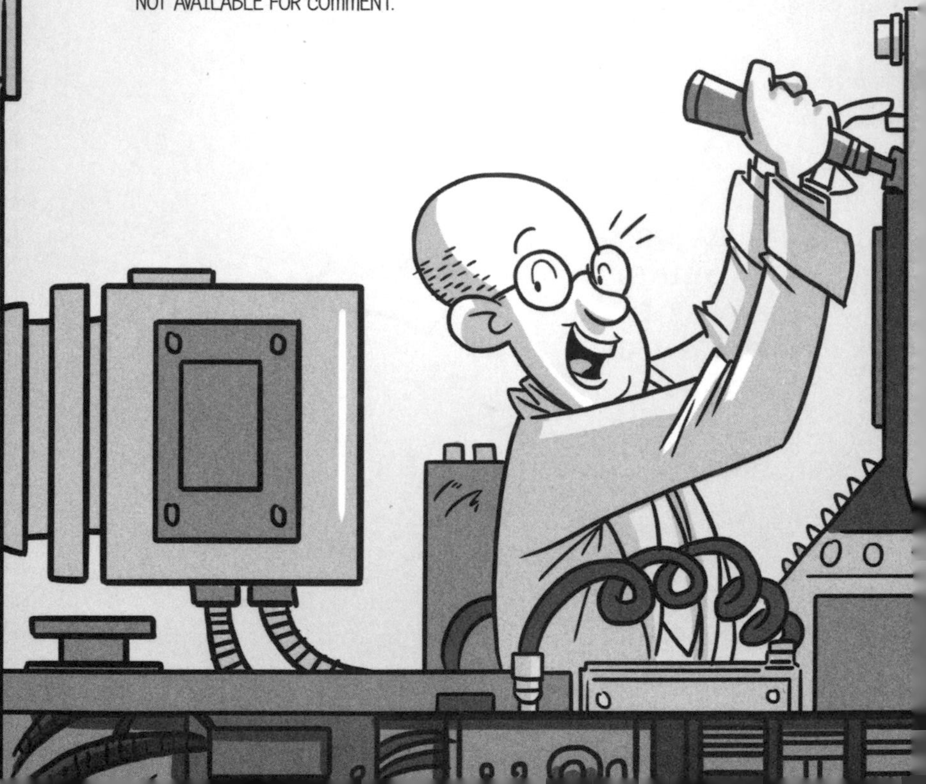

ILLUSTRATORS

DOUGLAS HOLGATE

IS A FREELANCE ILLUSTRATOR, COMIC BOOK ARTIST, AND CARTOONIST BASED IN MELBOURNE, AUSTRALIA. HIS WORK HAS BEEN PUBLISHED ALL AROUND THE WORLD BY RANDOM HOUSE, SIMON AND SCHUSTER, THE NEW YORKER MAGAZINE, MAD MAGAZINE, IMAGE COMICS, AND MANY OTHERS. HIS WORKS FOR CHILDREN INCLUDE THE ZINC ALLOY AND BIKE RIDER SERIES (CAPSTONE), SUPER CHICKEN NUGGET BOY (HYPERION), AND A NEW SERIES OF POPULAR SCIENCE BOOKS BY DR. KARL KRUSZELNICKI (PAN MACMILLAN). DOUGLAS HAS SPORTED A POWERFUL, MANLY BEARD SINCE AGE 12 (PROBABLY NOT TRUE) AND IS ALSO A PRETTY RAD DUDE (PROBABLY TRUE).

DARYLL COLLINS

IS A FREELANCE CARTOONIST WHOSE WORK HAS APPEARED IN BOOKS, MAGAZINES, COMIC STRIPS, ADVERTISING, GREETING CARDS, PRODUCT PACKAGING AND CHARACTER DESIGN. HE ENJOYS MUSIC, MOVIES, BASEBALL, FOOTBALL, COFFEE, PIZZA, PETS, AND OF COURSE... CARTOONS!

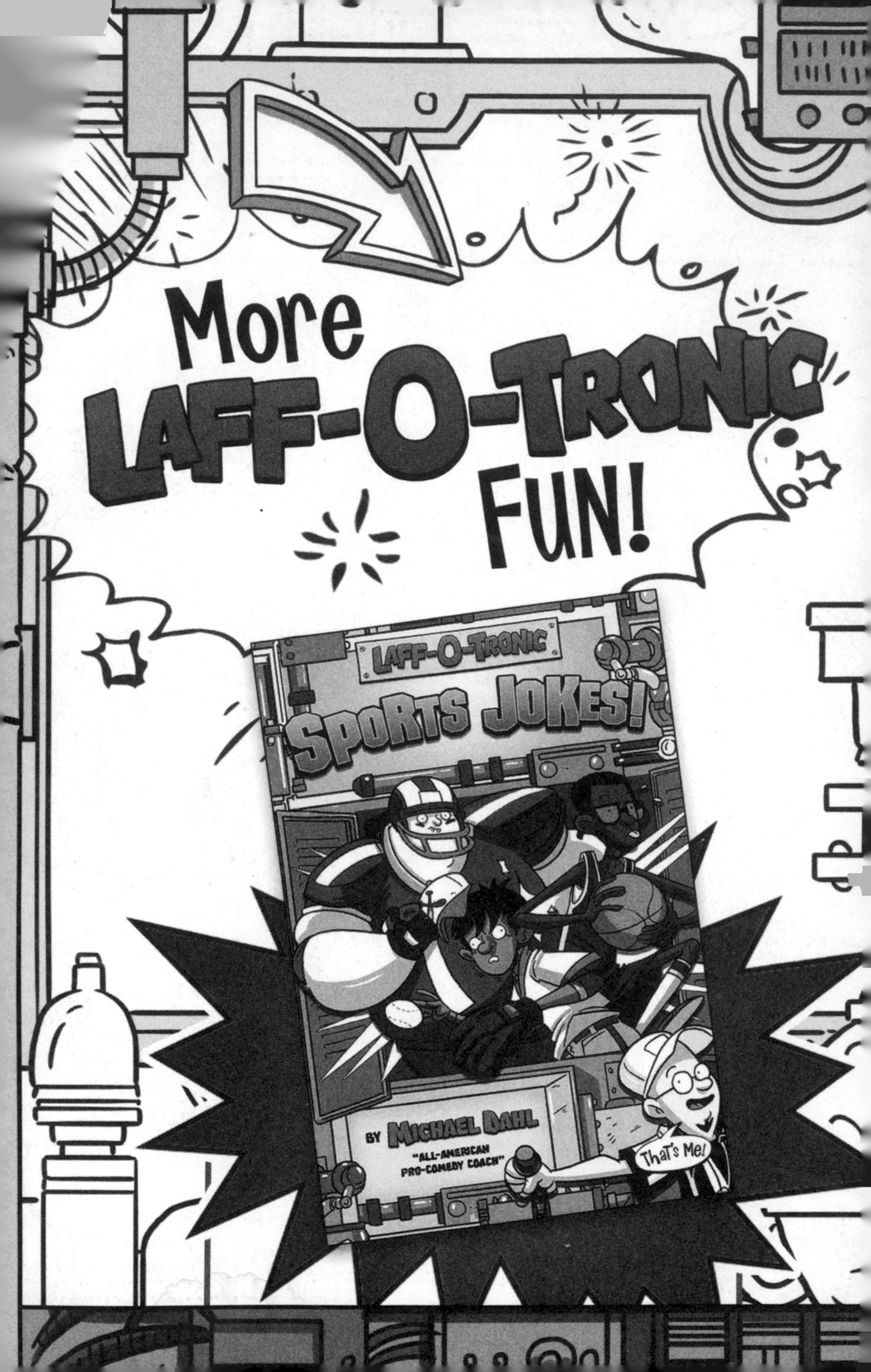
More LAFF-O-TRONIC FUN!
LAFF-O-TRONIC
SPORTS JOKES!
BY MICHAEL DAHL
"ALL-AMERICAN PRO-COMEDY COACH"
That's Me!

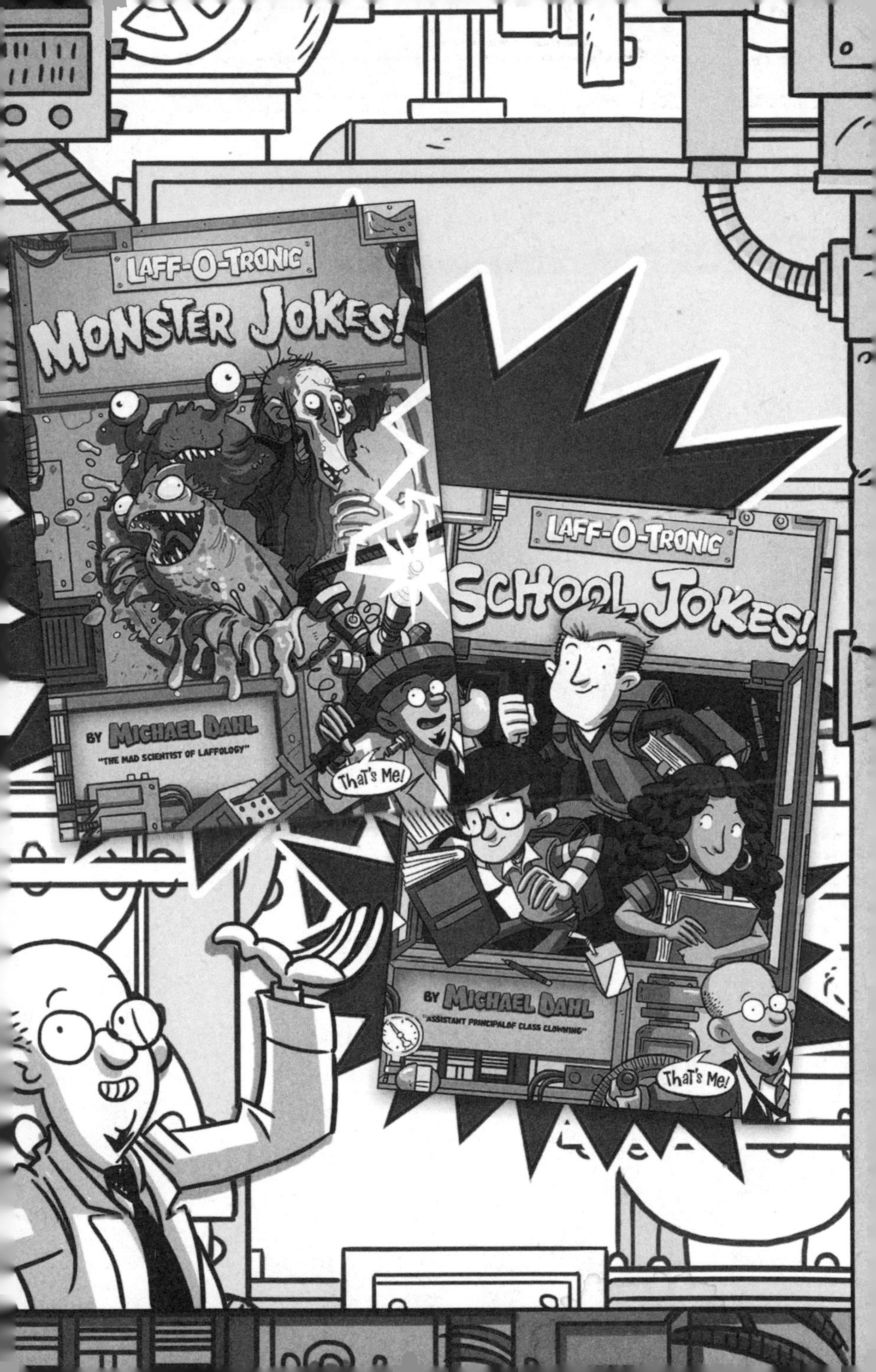
LAFF-O-TRONIC
MONSTER JOKES!
BY MICHAEL DAHL
"THE MAD SCIENTIST OF LAFFOLOGY"
That's Me!
LAFF-O-TRONIC
SCHOOL JOKES!
BY MICHAEL DAHL
"ASSISTANT PRINCIPALOF CLASS CLOWNING"
That's Me!

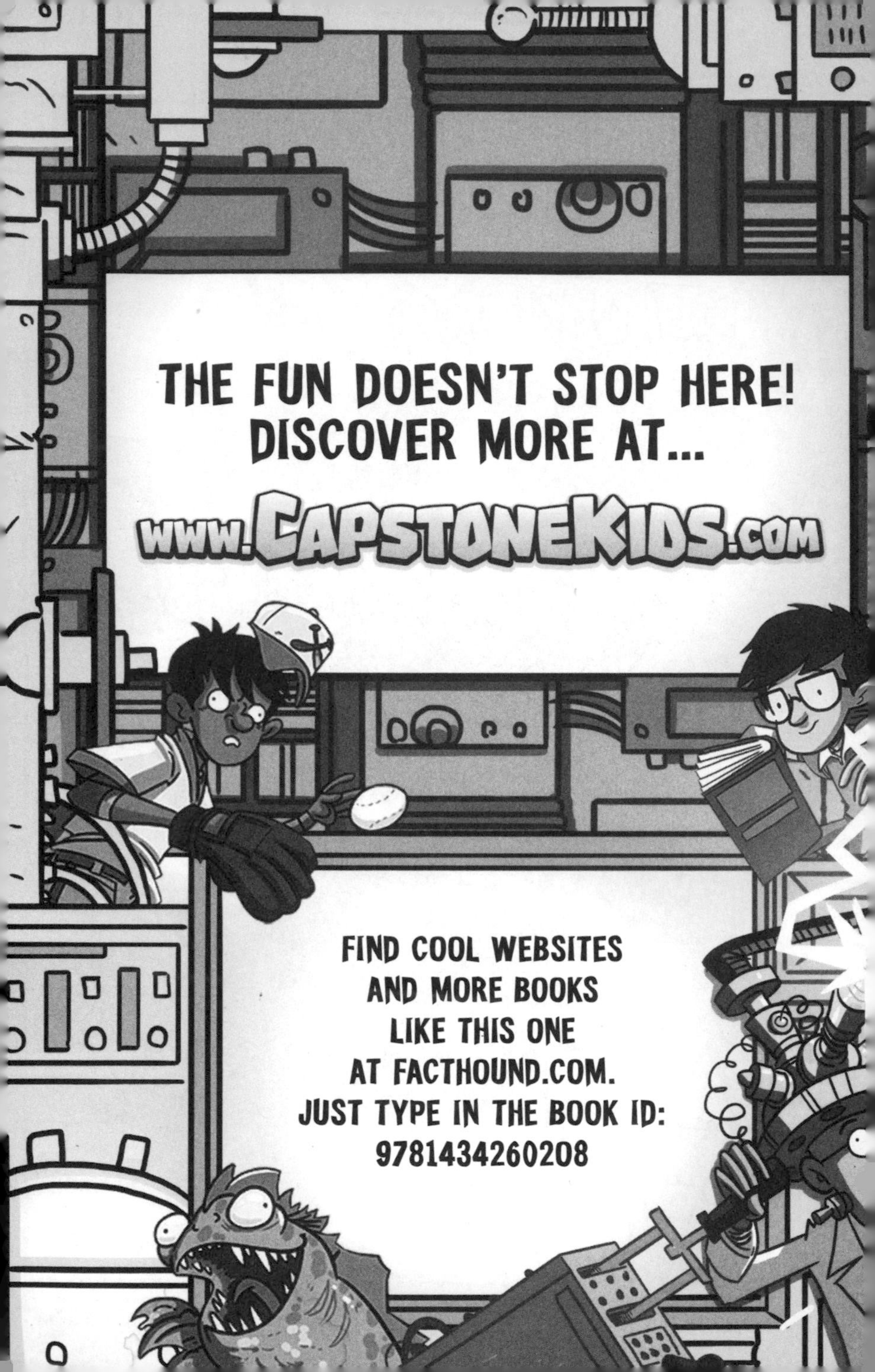
THE FUN DOESN'T STOP HERE!
DISCOVER MORE AT...
WWW.CAPSTONEKIDS.COM
FIND COOL WEBSITES
AND MORE BOOKS
LIKE THIS ONE
AT FACTHOUND.COM.
JUST TYPE IN THE BOOK ID:
9781434260208